When A Thug Falls For A Rich Girl 3

BY: MONIK

Synopsis

While Lamar And Anna is trying to get back on track with their lives. Anna decided to test Lamar's love for her she can't seem to figure out what to do since her kids have been kidnapped. Lamar is losing his mind trying to find his kids. While Ken and Jenn is off to a rough start trying to figure out the love they have for each other.

When Anna and Lamar finally feel like they have got they lives back on track something keeps on knocking them off of the horse. With Anna keeping secrets from Lamar and Ken keeping Secrets from Jenn will their secrets break them apart or bring them together even more.

Will they have the happier ever after?

Dedications

I would love to thank everybody that I know and that is in my life I don't think I could have did this and started writing with all of you all if I say I love you or go above and beyond for you then thank you. To all of my brother and sister it is so many of us I'm not naming all of yall but I may be using yall names in a few books so be on the lookout. To my mother Loretta and father Richard I love yall dearly. To my best friends, D&BO I LOVE YALL CRAZY ASSES. To my kids, Corey& Sa'Maya there isn't a day where I'm not thankful for you two being my blessing on this earth just know that I grind the way I do for you too. I would like to thank all my readers for your support. Thank you to my Publisher Thai for actually believing in me and taking a chance on me and being so cool I wouldn't want to be signed to anyone else. To my pen sisters yall are CRAZY but I wouldn't trade yall for nothing. I wanna also dedicate this my daughter who passed away Seven years ago and gave me one of my blessing and that's our baby girl I wish you could be here to see her grow up. But she is you in every form so rest easy. And we will always love you and since this is coming out on your bday its only right.

Craig D Ainsworth

April,2 1983- August 23,2010

Lekenndrick J Beene

July 1,1992- January 15, 2016

To the one that has my attention right now just know I appreciate you for trying..........

Table of Contents

Chapter 1 Lamar

I can't believe this shit is happening to me, my fucking girl and family. My wife is losing her mind and I can't find my damn kids. It's been a whole damn three months and I still can't find my kids. Me and Anna haven't been seeing eye to eye she hasn't even been staying here in the house.

She packed her shit and got her own place right after the kids went missing. Anna was talking about she can't be around me because she feels like I should be doing more. When I'm out here busting my ass trying to find them. Yall I have been doing everything in my power to find our kids and she acting like I'm not so fuck Anna right now.

I had to send my mom and sister out to California because I didn't want or need shit happening to them. But let me re-introduce myself again my name is Lamar Williams; I'm one of the biggest drug connects in Atlanta. I'm well known for losing my fucking mind and cool.

The one thing I don't play around with is family and my nigga and money. This nigga josh has crossed the line with me. I don't know what that man has against me but as soon as I find him I'm not giving him the opportunity to explain himself to me at all. Well I had to step down from the drug empire and handed it over to Ken cause my fucking mind is not right at the moment at all. Oh but trust I'm still in fucking charge and getting paid, I'm just not in the front line of it all anymore. I had to hire someone to run my stores and everything. The only thing I did every day was smoke, drink and kill that was it.

"Hey Lamar you down here" ken asked yelling my damn name

"Yea body I'm in here come on down" I hollered out

"So nigga you are about to stay in this room today or what?" ken asked looking at me as he walked into my office that has turned into my room I barley left out of here

"Nigga! I'm about to stay in this fucking room until the black team call me with a body that may have a lead to where the fuck my kids are"

"Are you fucking serious Lamar! Nigga you are on your way to jail my nigga if you don't start to think straight. I don't give a fuck how much money you got, how many people you have on the payroll. That is not going to stop the fucking police from kicking in your fucking door; you would know that shit if you picked up the phone for Carlos." Ken said while taking a seat next to me.

"So what Ken guess what I don't give a fuck. I want my kid's nigga, I want my wife and until I get that shit I'm killing any and everything all day every day." I said while throwing back a shot of Hennessey.

"Look Lamar you my nigga shit your damn near my brother and all. I'm not in your shoes so I don't know what you are going through, I don't know how you feeling right now at the moment. What I do know is that the way you are out here moving and going about this shit is wrong. Your lady is out here in these streets doing what the fuck she wants too. All the while trying to drag my fucking lady down with her and I'll be damned. So you need to get your stanky ass off this couch out of this room so you can do what only Lamar can do best and that's being a fucking Boss!"

"Ken I hear you my nigga and all but right now I can't control Anna man her mom is still out there. I can't find her or my kids I feel like less than a man. Right now, I don't know what to do but kill people so let me do me and you do what you do best and that's run them streets but ill deal with Anna through for sure so don't worry about her."

"Just don't put your hands on that girl Mar."

"Man, Ken she should be here like me waiting to put a bullet in somebody but naw man she is out in these damn streets doing good knows what and I'm supposed to let that shit pass naw I don't think so now I won't put my hands on her ass but don't hold me responsible for my actions when I catch her dumb as doing something".

"Alright man look I'm gone call me if you need me cause talking to your crazy ass is pointless right now".

I watched this nigga Ken leave out my house, before I went upstairs to my room to get dressed. I needed to find Anna ass before the day was over, and make her bring her ass back home. Enough was a fucking enough. When my brother felt the need to check me about my own damn wife, shyt was about to change.

I didn't listen to many people, but what Ken was saying to me made all the fucking sense in the world. I went to the control panel that Anna had me put in the house, and turned on the Mozzy station on Pandora, that's all I listen to at the moment. I felt like that man was speaking to my soul, and knew how to get me in the right frame of mind.

I grabbed my all black True Religion jeans with a shirt to match, and my new Jordan's. Once I made my way to the shower, did what I had to do, I made sure I had my black diamond earrings in my ear with my black diamond chain, and watch to match on.

I grabbed both of my phones, with my Audi keys, yea I know what ya'll thinking I didn't need a new car, but oh fucking well I'm depressed. I have money so I'm going to spend it as I see fit. After I made it to the car, and on my way, I needed to get me something to eat, because I can't even remember the last time I ate.

So I pulled up, and into the nearest chick-fill-A. I got my normal, a spicy chicken sandwich meal, with an extra sandwich. Yea I know I'm greedy as hell lol, but whatever I was hungry. I didn't even realize it until I was on the highway, and noticed that I had already smacked the two sandwiches, and killed the whole soda.

So yeah, I guess a nigga was starving. I was making my way to Anna lil house to see what the fuck she has been up too, So I can find out what the fuck Ken was talking about. As I made my way to the eastside, I pulled up to Anna house already pissed off.

"Man! I swear I don't have time for this shit"

I said to no one, but myself since I was the only one in this damn car. I hopped out the car, and headed for Anna door. Now yall, I know I'm not hearing what I think I am hearing? Is this bitch in this house that I'm paying for the fucking next nigga? I walked through the house to find where the sounds were coming from. I walked towards the downstairs bedroom that was located in the back of the house. I instantly grabbed my gun from under my shirt in the back, I pushed the door open, stood there, and watched the woman that I love fucking on the next nigga.

"So, Anna this the way we rocking now? Cause if so let me know, so I can go find me a bad bitch to fuck tonight" I asked shocking the fuck out of her.

"OMG! Lamar what are you doing here?

Before I could even answer her dumb ass question, I went straight for the nigga "See what you got me doing Anna? Out here killing niggas, cause you wanna be a fucking hoe, Aye nigga my fucking wife is off limits! Do you know who the fuck I am young blood? Don't look her way my, nigga she can't save your life right now"

"Lamar please stop! Let him go please!" Anna begged me

"Naw Anna, this is what you wanted right well here you go" after beating this nigga ass for what seemed like forever, and seeing his lifeless body on the hardwood floor, I called my team to come and clean this shit, and get her shit out of this house.

"So, this the type of woman and wife you wanna be huh?" I asked looking at Anna like I wanted to kill her ass next. She could tell just by looking at me.

"No! I don't Lamar I just didn't sign up for this life style, and now my kids are missing you haven't been talking to me, and barley fucking me. So, what did you think was going to happen? Lamar, you over here killing niggas and shit like, what the fuck!"

"Anna, you over here fucking niggas, like what the fuck you want me to do huh! You know what Anna, go get your shit. Let's go right now, before you be just like that nigga on this fucking floor. Try it if you want to, I'm the last nigga on this earth you wanna be playing with right now".

I walked off leaving her ass naked in the room crying, she knows she fucked up, but that's my wife. I can't just leave her, I can't, and won't give up on her or my marriage. Like my father did my mother, I just won't, but that don't make it right either. I went to the car to wait for her silly ass, while my team pulled up to clear up the place. If she thought she was going to keep doing this shit, she had another thing coming. I was about to have her with two of my niggas, with her ass at all times no matter if she like it or not.

Chapter 2 Anna

So, I know yall just read that bullshit, so here I am in this house in the room with guards standing by the fucking door. I feel like I'm being held hostage, and against my own fucking will, but oh well that's my husband. As much as I want this, I need to get my life together. Ever since my kids went missing, I haven't been the same person. I've been buying pills, and popping them all the time. I just want my life back, but let me re-introduce myself my name is Anna Williams. Now I am married to one of the biggest drug connects in Atlanta. I was born and raised here, I am a spoiled rich girl that was just fucked over by her father and Mother, I learned that I had a sister that was my best friend. I've gained a whole new fucking family, and had two kids. I haven't been able to get my houses up and running, because I really don't give a fuck about much right about now. All I want is my kids back, and this nigga that it seemed like everybody feared, can't even find them. So, I was about to take matters into my own hands, I knew I wasn't going anywhere with my two new fucking shadows so I needed to make everything I do count. Tomorrow was going to be the first day, I really start looking. I grabbed my laptop off of my nightstand, and my notebook with a pen with my phone. I was looking for the best private detective there was in this big ass city.

Once I had found who I felt good about paying for this job, I called his number that was located on his website.

"Hello, this is private wonders, my name is Victoria how may we serve you today?"

"Hello, my name is Mrs. Williams, and I'm seeking to find my two kids. So, can you point me in the right direction please" I asked as nicely as I could.

"Okay well Mr. Smith will be able to take your call now, so just hold on a few seconds, and I'll pass you through just please hold on".

After waiting on the line for what seemed like forever, I was finally being connected to this Mr. Smith guy

"Hello Mrs. Williams, I'm sorry for the long wait, I was finishing up a phone call".

"Hello, and that is fine. I just need to know if you can find my kids?" I asked getting straight to the point.

"Well okay, I can surely do my best, so why don't you tell me everything from start to finish. Don't leave anything out, and if I happen to just get quiet while your speaking, just know that I'm taking notes okay. After we can then set up a meeting for tomorrow afternoon for payment, and I can give you any information I find out from now to then. Is that okay"

"Yes, that is fine by me". Two fucking hours later I gave him all Lamar and I information. Phone numbers, addresses, and any and everything he asked for. I had a meeting setup with him for tomorrow, this man fee was crazy, but I'll pay all the money in the world to go get my kids back. I closed my laptop, put all my things back up, and cleaned my bed back up. Yall I had papers all over the bed. I really don't know what Lamar been doing, because he hasn't told me shit, like at all. That's my fucking husband, he has been talking to yall the whole time, but anyway I grabbed me one of Lamar big ass shirts, and went and ran me a hot ass bath. I turned on my

Pandora on my wall, lol Lamar didn't understand why I needed my music, but hopefully he will understand one day. That shit keep me from fucking up everything in my path, while my water was running I decide to call Jenn. I haven't talked to her in like a week, now that she is with Ken I haven't seen too much of her.

"Hey sis/best friend what you doing?" I asked sitting back on the edge of the tub

"Hey Hoe, I'm at the house where you at? And what you doing?" Jenn asked

"Shit, Lamar came and got me from the house. He fucked off my side piece, so now I'm locked in this damn room at the house with two guards standing by the door".

"Hahaha, are you fucking serious right now? What the fuck do you mean fucked off your side piece?"

"Well you know I had lil baby on the side since all this shit happened, and I guess Lamar had, had a little bird in his fucking ear girl, cause that nigga came to the other house, and put that man to bed if you know what I mean. That's why I'm locked in this damn room now" I said hearing Jenn laughing at me

"Girl I told you that nigga Lamar is fucking crazy, and has been losing his fucking mind since the twins went missing. Have you heard anything yet about the babies?

"Naw sis, I haven't, but I need a favor from you. I need you to come get me tomorrow, because I have a meeting with a private investigator at the factory. I just don't want Lamar finding out, so I need you to take me please Jenn?" I asked damn near begging.

"Are you bat shit crazy Anna! Because you must be, them niggas are going to kill us. Do you know who we fuck with, because I think you have forgotten. Well let me refresh your memory, Lamar and Kenndrick two of the craziest nigga's in Atlanta"

"Jenn, look I know so just be here...Damn! I'm trying to find my kids so either you in or out, but trust me I will be there so come get me at twelve tomorrow okay and thank you in advance"

"Got damned I just had to hang up in her face I couldn't believe she was acting like that right now of all times when I need her the most. I grabbed my towel and made my way back into the bathroom. I can't believe this is my life and I'm married who would of thought? As I slipped into the water I closed my eyes and let the bath bombs I dropped them into the water dissolve, while the music take my mind away to another place than the one I'm in at the moment".

Chapter 3 Lamar

So, I'm in my office trying to calm my fucking nerves I can't believe I just caught my wife fucking somebody else. Yall please believe me when I say; this shit is out of control, like it's really out of hand, so I had two of my men at her side at all times. I had a few things to get done today I need to go to the warehouse and back to that fuck ass hospital. I also had a meeting with my dude Carlos yall remember him he is on the police force. Yeah, I had cops on my payroll shit who didn't. I made my way upstairs so I can see Anna before I left for the night see yall…unlike my wife I'm not trying to step out of this marriage, but you nor I can't get that shit through her fucking head.

"what's up boss" one of the guards said as he seen me approaching the door.

"Nothing much I'm about to be out most of the night I have three other men coming to the house to watch it I want someone in the front, in the back, and someone watching all cameras. Anna don't leave this house at all! Yall got it?"

"yeah, we hear you"

As I stepped inside the room to talk to Anna or see what she was up too I heard Pandora going I swear this lady was crazy about music, I stepped inside the bathroom and seen Anna sitting in the tub sound asleep I swear yall I missed my fucking wife and this moment reminded me why I can't live my life without her. I sat my phone down by the sink as I walked over to the tub just to find her fast asleep in the water. This was the normal thing for Anna. I grabbed her towel she had laid out by the tub so I can get her out and lay her in the bed hoping she didn't wake up. She was light as a fucking feather she has definitely lost some weight since all of this drama unfolded.

"Lamar what are you doing?" Anna asked

"I'm putting you in the bed Ma you fell asleep in the tub and the water was cold as hell" so I took you out the water…is that okay for me to do?

"I'm sorry babe I just want my kids back, my life back,I'm losing my mind and I promise you I won't step out of our marriage again" Anna said as I was laying her down on the bed

"I forgive you Ma but just know that I will kill you and the nigga next time! now get some sleep I have a few thigs to do so I will be back in a few hours okay".

"Okay Lamar please don't cheat on me"

I must have stopped dead in my tracks as I was walking out the room and turned to face her.

"Are you fucking serious right now?" I asked

"Yes, Lamar I am"

"Naw Ma! You can't be serious I just caught you fucking one of my corner boys and I had to kill that nigga Ma in a house that I'm paying for and you have the nerve to fix your nasty ass mouth that you probably used to suck that nigga dick with…so take your nasty ass back the fuck to sleep while I go out and try to get a step closer to finding our kids."

I couldn't even believe that she just came at me for real. I love my wife I just can't fuck with her right now. Once I made my way out the house to the damn hospital I had already been in a bad state of mind and I just knew someone was about to catch the short end of the stick. After I found me a parking space, I had to meet up with the head of security to get the information for that nurse, I was hoping he had an address on file for her. I stepped inside the emergency room where I was told to meet him at, I spotted him almost instantly.

"what's good Mont?"

"Shit I can't call it but let's go inside my office so we can talk"

I followed this bubble gum as nigga to his office but I was more than ready to end this nigga life if he wanted to try me in any shape form or fashion.

"So, what can you tell me that I don't already know and I don't have all damn night man" I said as soon as he closed his office door.

"Well here is the file you needed the girl name is Brittney Jones I also had my guy dig a little deeper so you can have a little more information on her" he said sitting down in his chair like he was that nigga

"Thanks man so what about the video's?"

"Yeah, I got this for you as well, here you go, do you have the payment?"

"Man, I swear you lil niggas really be trying me" I said reaching inside my coat to get this nigga money. This nigga was charging me eight grand per item.

"Here you go and next time don't act like you pressed for that punk ass change you asking for because Men like

myself don't and will not respect that kind of shit got it?"
I said walking out of that man office and headed back to
my car to go to the warehouse to talk to Carlos about this
information.

I pulled into the same as parking space as always. I could
tell who was here just by the cars that were parked
outside, that crazy ass nigga Ken was here as always,
Carlos was here and a few of our men were here as well.

I made my way inside and straight to the video room we
had with Ken and Carlos right behind me on my heels.

"What's up brody" Ken said walking into the room

"Shit I can't call it, I just left the hospital and got that
information I needed so here Carlos that is everything
that I got from him and that you will need you have 24
hours from now to get me more information because I'm

ready to end this shit once and for all."

"Yeah bro I hear you but I got some shit to holla at you about tho" Ken said while he was taking a seat next to me

"So? Speak your mind lil bro get that shit off your chest" I said

"See you a straight shooter and I don't hold my tongue and I don't want no one around me to either"

"Alright well look, I heard Jenn and Ana on the phone earlier and it seems like Anna has hired a private Investigator and they are supposed to be meeting tomorrow at the Factory" Ken said

"Okay so she is trying...?" is all I could say

"So, you cool with that we don't need no outsiders in this we can find the kids our self brody" Ken said trying to convince me

"I hear you but look my kids been missing and been gone for three months so whatever he can do I'm willing to accept at the moment so can you let Carlos know his name and information so he can check him out too"

"Alright bro I got you are you going back to the house tonight with Anna or what?"

"Yeah I might just not sure yet but look we good here I'm about to watch all of these videos and I'll call you a lil later and let you know if I found out anything else"

"Alright big bro I got you I'm going to slide by the traps really quick to do some pickups"

I watched my bro leave and I turned my attention back to the monitors I can't believe this is what my life has become.

Chapter 4 Josh

Meanwhile across town

" Man! Brittney can you shut them damn kids up already they've been crying for damn near a fucking hour" Josh yelled at Brittney as she tried to calm the twins down.

"Nigga if you would have followed the fucking plan we wouldn't be in this fucked up situation now what you need to do is find a way to give that man his kids back and get that money so we can get the fuck out of Atlanta nigga before we both end up dead I should have never let you talk or dick me down into some dumb ass bullshit like this"

"Bitch who you talking too I know what the fuck I did and what the fuck I need to do but you don't know what the fuck that nigga Lamar is capable of so calm the fuck down okay bitch and just try to shut them fuck ass babies up"

"Nigga that is what you been saying for the longest and the last three months get this done or I'm taking them to the fucking fire station and you have been able to get a fucking dime out of him because I'm not losing my life over these two crybabies"

"Or else what Brittney don't you realize that even if you did do some shit like that he will still find you and kill your ass first so why don't you just put them kids to sleep then come and suck this dick like I taught you too" I heard that trick smack her lips as she walked away like I knew she would at the thought of wrapping her lips around my dick, but anyway let me tell yall who the fuck I am in case yall forgot lol my name is Josh I'm six foot two even light skin fade with light brown eyes with a body any chick would want a piece of but enough of that back to this fuck ass story so I've been knowing Lamar since him and his family moved on the block. Me, Lamar and Ken became the best of friends. Shit the best team on the block, we been riding for each other ever since, but I grew a hatred for Lamar when the big homie gave up his shit and his whole entire operation over to this nigga Lamar. I've been trying to get at this nigga for the longest and now that I finally got the nigga by the balls that's the way it's going to stay now I don't know what to do about these kids, but I need to figure out a way to get them the fuck out my house and far the fuck away from me. I can't call that nigga Ken cause I know he took

Lamar side over mine and I've been knowing the nigga longer the that nigga. Hell we was more like brothers than anything…I need to figure out how to get this Money and get them the fuck out of Atlanta.

"Well them damn kids are sleep so have you figured out a way to get rid of them fuck ass kids yet" Brittney asked while taking my dick out of my boxers and falling to her knees to give me some good sloppy, I watched her wrap her lips around my dick, as she made her mouth extra wet. Brittney was downright nasty she took sloppy toppy to a different height and she had a doctrine in swallowing kids. Brittney spit on my dick then swirled her tongue around my dick "fuck girl!" I exclaimed.

Brittney attacked my dick like an anaconda on its prey. "Oh shit!" I grabbed the back of her head as my toes was doing they own dance. See this is the shit that be having me come back for more. I had to think about Hella bull shit to keep from bussing too soon. But that shit didn't work because soon as Brittney started gagging on purpose I grabbed her tracks and started fucking her throat with no mercy all my kids went down the walls of her throat as I nutted in her mouth.

"Josh why the fuck did you do that nasty as shit just because I suck your dick like that don't mean I like or love to swallow" Brittney yelled at me

"Oh well you might as well get used to it cause I will never stop doing it" I got up and fixed my clothes with Brittney sitting on the floor looking stupid I grabbed my keys and wallet off the table and headed to my little warehouse to make a few calls I figured out that I was going to run in all this nigga trap houses and just take all his money and dope I know he passed everything over to ken so I know that nigga changed everything so I was going to call one of my niggas that was still on the payroll and see if he could be bought.

I pulled up to the warehouse twenty min later to speak to this nigga about getting this money.

"What's good Earnest" I said to the nigga as I walked up to him

"Shit, lets gets this shit over with so I can go on about my day" Earnest said while stepping inside my office and taking a seat in front of my desk.

"So why don't you tell me everything I need to know about the way Ken is running things now since Lamar handed things over" I said

"Are you serious my nigga I should out a bullet between your fucking eyes right now and if I knew anything I still wouldn't tell you shyt that's number one and number two my nigga I don't know shit because that nigga doesn't tell us shyt but what we need to know Ken and Lamar keep that shyt to themselves so if that's the reason why you called me here then I suggest you go and fuck yourself." I watch this nigga pull out his gun a sat it in his lap I'm not understanding why this nigga was still be sitting here in my fucking face and office if he wasn't going to tell me shyt.

"Then why the fuck are you still sitting in my fucking presence then nigga" I watched this nigga get up and walk out my warehouse and I knew as soon as he stepped out the door I knew I had fucked up Lamar and Ken had a loyal team and loyal men by their side and it was only a matter of time before them niggas come knocking down my door I needed to get the fuck out of town and fucking quick. I grabbed all of my shit off of my desk and headed

back to the house to figure this shyt out with Brittney.

******

Chapter 5 Anna

I woke up to find out that Lamar never came home last night, what was the fucking point of bringing me back here if this nigga wasn't going to be here with me.

Whatever, yall know that man better than I do at this point, I grabbed my phone and sent Jenn a text message letting her know to be ready and to get her as here on time.

I got out of the bed and walked over to the closet to grab me something simple to wear I didn't want to overdo it at all.

It was almost time to go and Jenn have yet to arrive I swear if the bitch didn't want to come then that's all she had to say I sometime wish Ketta was around so she could help me but fucking Lamar sent her and his mom to California while all this is going on.

At least I have the men to go with me if I needed them I grabbed my purse and keys even though I knew I wouldn't be driving at all anymore and headed downstairs.

"thing one and thing two yall ready I got places to be and things to do so I need to go to the factory first and then I guess the mall after that is that's cool with yall" I said

"Boss lady we will take you anywhere you need to go today okay so which car will you like to take today?"

"Hell, it doesn't matter let's just go already" I said

walking out the door

once we made it to the cheesecake factory and I checked

in and order my regular and waited I decided to call

Lamar and see what he was doing instead of sitting here

pulling my freaking hair out.

"Hey babe, what are you doing?"

"Oh, so now I'm babe and the better question is what the

hell are you doing?"

"Lamar I swear don't answer a freaking question with a

question you know I hate that shit I'm trying to be nice

here so give me a damn break"

"Look Ma I don't need you to be nice to me I need you to

step up and be my fucking wife and help me find our

babies that's what I need you to do now can you handle

that Ma?"

"Yeah Lamar I got you, are you coming home tonight or are you staying with a hoe tonight?"

"Look Anastasia I'm not fucking around on you okay my dick won't even get hard for the next bitch okay now where are you at? And what the fuck are you doing Ma?"

"I'm at the Cheesecake factory meeting with a private Investigator to see if he can help us find the twins so do you have any information that I can give him to help?"

"Naw Ma I don't but thank you for taking Actions Babe I really do appreciate it and I love you even more for this but once we find the kids we need to get back to us and go on a vacation or something okay?"

"Okay Lamar that's good and all but look they guy is walking up to the table so I'll call you when I'm done and let you know what he says okay babe?"

I think I hung up on him before he even said bye the man walking toward me was something kind of handsome he had to be about six 'five at best dark chocolate skin that looked like it tasted so damn good he had waves for days and a body out of this world and I didn't see no damn ring on his finger unlike my own you couldn't miss this big ass rock on my hand.

"Hello Mrs., Williams I'm Mr. Smith nice to put a voice to a face and I see you have gotten lunch started without me"

"Well it's nice to meet you as well you are so not what I was expecting so excuse me if I seemed shacked and you know it's never nice to keep a woman waiting so why don't we just get down to business alright!"

"Well a woman that knows what she wants, okay well let me get a drink and pull out my surprise and we can get started okay?"

I couldn't take my eyes off this man I watched him get out all of his things out of his bag and set up I could just imagine his hands all over my body… okay I need to snap the fuck out of it and focus on why the fuck I'm here.

"Okay so can you tell me more about your information about your babies?"

once I explained him everything that happen from the start to finish he damn near had a whole notebook full of shit and had me crying with people looking at me like I was crazy.

"So, is that all you need from me?" I asked as I was whipping my eyes and getting my stuff ready to leave.

"Well yes that would be all and I'll be in touch with you

in a few days and I promise you I'm going to do everything I can to help you find your kids for you"

I just looked at him and nodded my head on my way out the fucking door I definitely need to go spend some money after that bullshyt meeting I just had.

Once I got to the car I called Jenn "So where the fuck you was at and why the fuck didn't you come with me I really needed you sis"

"Anna, I know but this was something you needed to do for you and Lamar I won't always be there or around Anna you my girl hell and now my sister. I'll be here for you but something like this you need to do on your own but how did it go?"

"Hell, it went ok the dude said he is going to try to do everything he can to find the kids now I have thing one and thing two driving me to the mall so I can spend some of Lamar's money can you at least come to the damn mall with me or are you too busy?"

"Naw I can meet you there I'm leaving the house so I'll meet you in the food court I promise oh and I need for you to sign a few papers too because we have a few new kids coming to the houses on Monday"

"Okay just bring the papers with you and I'll see you at the mall I need to call Lamar and let him know how it went"

"Alright love" once I hung up I knew I needed to call Lamar but instead I just sent him a text message letting him know that we needed to talk tonight when we both got home and I love him. I slid my phone back into my purse and waited until we got to the mall.

Chapter 6 Jenn

So yall know who I am by this time I'm Anna best friend and Sister now that we found out we have the same fuck ass father but moving on. My life hasn't been the same since and now I'm in a relationship with Kenndrick aka Ken and he has taken over the streets since Lamar has stepped down and I'm not too happy with that shit but hell I can't do shyt about that.

Now I was supposed to meet up with Anna to go meet a private Investigator but that was her issue and not mine. I know I sound fucked up and all but I've been living behind Anna's shadow all my life and that shit was over from this day forward, I was running the girls and boys home that she wanted to start, now we really have no fucking involvement at all. Ketta was running her part from California and we were planning on opening up two more homes for kids in California, L.A to be exact so she was handling all that from where she was.

I called ken to let him know I was on my way to the mall to meet up with Anna so we could talk and I can have her sign her papers and then changed my clothes to my normal look all black is what I love to wear so my all black true Religion outfit and my red Timbs is what I decided to wear today I paired it with my Gucci watch and rings and earrings that Ken just bought me last week yea see that is the best part of being with a King because he treats me like the freaking Queen that I am.

Once I was dressed I eyed myself in the mirror "damn

I'm fine I could fuck myself" yea I said it don't act like yall don't wanna fuck yall self sometimes.

I grabbed my keys to my new Range Rover see I told yall being treated like a Queen.

Thirty-nine minutes later I was pulling up to the mall I grabbed my Birkin bag with the papers I needed Anna to sign then made my way to the food court. I looked around and spotted Anna sitting in the back like she was hiding from someone.

"Girl why the fuck is you all the way back here looking like you hiding for your life?" I questioned why I laughed at her

"Girl no reason I'm just not in the mood and I need to shop till my feet hurt I know there is some new Jordan's that came out that I want the kids, Lamar, and I to have.

And just a few outfits but I wanna get Lamar some jewelry too.

"Alright well here is the papers I need you to sign here at the bottom of each page"

"Okay so what is all this for again Jenn?"

"Well if you must know now it's so we can open up two more houses in California while Ketta is out there with mom" so yall reading this can imagine how I'm looking at her right now because the last time I checked this was our business and now she is making me feel like I don't have the right to make the decision about what we do for business and it seems like she has an issue with me and Ketta running things and making plans without her now I know she lying.

"well since you and Ketta are making all the fucking

plans why don't yall just buy me out?" Anna said looking like her feeling are hurt

"Really Anna so because shyt is not your way right now you wanna act like a spoiled bitch because you're not getting your way well let me tell you something this big ass world don't resolve around your little ass okay so grow the fuck up and figure it the hell out, your damn kids are MISSING! Right now for Christ sake and you're in a fucking mall shopping instead of being a rider and standing by Lamar side and looking for your fucking kids my niece and nephew and god kids I swear you don't deserve Lamar ass" I watched Anna sit there looking dumb founded as I grabbed my shit and made my way back out the mall I swear I didn't need this shit at the moment and someone needed to tell her about her damn self and I guess I was the woman to do it fuck I needed to call Ken and let him know I swear I feel like moving to L.A got dammit I think I just might go on a very long vacation hell I need a break from life I can't keep doing or living like this shyt.

I see ken car in my driveway once I pulled up and I swear I wasn't ready for this conversation see yall are probably like what Ken has to do with this see Ken and Lamar are tighter than glue and if something is up with Lamar then Ken has to put his two cents in it and I'm pretty sure Anna cry baby ass has called Lamar as soon as I walked off so here we go with this bullshit.

"Ken baby you here?" I called out as I sat my bags down in the kitchen and made my way to the basement.

"Babe where you at why you got me calling your fucking name throughout the house where you at?"

The only noise I heard was fucking noises now I know this dirty dick as nigga didn't think it would be cool to fuck a bitch in my house well our house I know he didn't think that. But hell, I was wrong once stepped all the way in the room and all I seen was ass in the air and ken pumping away for his life.

"So, you fucking feel like it's okay to fuck hoes in our house ken!" I yelled while trying to get to the bitch.

"Shyt babe calm down calm the fuck down okay aye bitch get your shyt and I'll catch up with you later" ken said to the bitch

"Oh well now you wanna check on the bitch oh okay ken well you and this bitch can have this shit baby girl you don't have to leave because I will leave.

I ran up the stairs so freaking fast and to our supposedly

to be bedroom and started grabbing shit and trashing his shit "So you really wanna fuck other people huh well by all means necessary do you but you won't be tagging me along I got enough bullshit to deal with I don't have time for this Ken"!

Once I had everything I felt I needed I grabbed my keys off the table in the kitchen and left didn't plan on coming back anytime soon.

California here I come I sent Ketta a message letting her know I was on my way and I'll call her when I make it.

FUCK!!!! I yelled as I was driving to the airport this nigga really tried me yall.

Yo this can't really be my life who ever writing this can't be for real right now LMMFAO YALL CAN'T BE SERIOUS! I had to keep laughing from crying.........

Chapter 7 Ken

So yall read what just happen yeah, I was fucking a bitch in her house but hell she had been getting out lately and what did she think was going to happen, but Damn I didn't expect her to leave a nigga.

I just thought she would try and fight the bitch but instead she packed all her shyt and really left a nigga though. And fuck off my shyt while she was at it. On top of all that I got Lamar on my back about some stuff Jenn said to Anna today.

Well hell now I just need to find out where Jenn took her ass too. To try and get my girl back I'm not used to being without her. Once I got dressed and grab my phones I headed out of the house. I needed to go by all the traps and figure out how I can help Lamar with finding my god kids.

"Yo, Lamar Jenn just caught me fucking a chick in the house, and left me so I am about to go do some pick-ups and drop offs so do you need anything while I'm out brody."

"Well damn nigga that's a way to start off a phone conversation and yeah meet me at the house I got a few leads I want to go over it with you when you done."

I hopped in my car and drove over to the south side of Atlanta I had set up four new houses with school kids to work and live in them that was displaced. I got them off of the streets and taught them how to fend for themselves. One thing about the big bro that put me on to this street life always told me that if you give a man a fish he will eat for a day but if you teach a man how to fish he will eat for a lifetime.

Now I know yall are wondering why I haven't made a call to Jenn. It's because she needs her alone time and that is what I was going to give her for the time being. But damn Ya boy need some time as well and just as well as she is messed up behind my actions so am I.

So, I know when I did call her I had to have my shit in order and knew what I was going to say to her. My intentions are with her now don't get me wrong I do want to spend the rest of my life with her. I just don't know if I'm fully ready to do that.

Once I parked I looked around and seen all of the men working I was kind of proud. Is that a weird thing to say, hell yeah it is. But whatever, I got out of my truck and walked over to Marco house he was the one that was in charge of his house and was supposed to keep the young workers in line. But I think this nigga Marco was getting high on the product. And I was about to put an end to that shyt right now.

"hey boss do you have a min to chop it up for a second?" one of my new young niggas asked as I walked up on the house.

"yeah what's up and speak fast I got shyt to handle."

"well yesterday when I got my package that shyt came up short after Marco gave me my share to get off." I was looking at this lil boy like he was stupid

"so, what would you like to do to fix it since you wanna go run and tell on people?"

"naw big homie it wasn't like that at all I just don't want it to be my ass that's all I'm saying I put in the difference that would be missed out of it."

"so, if you did that what the fuck was the point telling me huh?" I had to ask

"I guess to just let you know."

"well let me tell you a few things if you feel something is off you handle that shit like a man you feel me things of that nature don't need to be brought to my attention but one thing you don't do is come running back to me with that shit don't ask don't tell shot first no questions asked now don't get me wrong lil nigga thanks for the info but there is nothing and I do mean nothing you can tell me about my houses or my product that I don't already know about now it's time for a meeting lets go and see what the others think about you speaking up."

As we walked in the house I could see the lil nigga

shaking in his shoes but the number one thing you don't do is give up information willing or not.

"Yo Marco meeting now round everyone up let's go." I said as I walked down into the basement I had it soundproofed so we could handle our business in peace. I was waiting for everyone to get here, five minutes later I was surrounded by my whole crew on the Southside.

"so, I bet yall is wondering why I got yall here I'm not going to make this shit a long speech. So, I was informed that a package was short now Marco is responsible. So Marco do you have a reason as to why this happen?

"Well"

"I'm guessing you don't so that's a no I take it and if you do I really don't give two fucks!"

I pulled out my 9mm and sent a bullet right between the

eyes, see I was a quick unlike Lamar I don't have time for the bullshit, or talking, I turned my gun to the new-found snitch.

"so, since you wanna go talking and telling you can join him."

All was said while the rest of the crew looked on scared shitless "let this be a lesson learned for yall if there is an issue I already know about it and if you wanna tell on anybody here kill your fucking self before I have to I already have too many bodies on my hands but don't get it fucked up ill chop all you niggas up and then pay for your funeral and I'll sit in the front row holding yall mamas hand now try it if yall want. Now Earnest will be taking over this house and if there is an issue let me know now." I looked around waiting for someone to speak up. "Alright well let me get my fucking money so I can get the fuck on." Once I collected my money I left on my way to the warehouse to meet up with Lamar I called earnest to let him know of the change and sent Jenn a text message I needed my lady back and it was about time I'd man the fuck up an do what I have to do and make her my wife I just need to speak to Anna and Lamar about this shit first.

Chapter 8 Lamar

I got a lead on my kids and it was time to go and handle that shit. The videos I got from the hospital showed me the girl leaving out of the hospital getting into a car and I was able to get a license plate number. So, I hit up my connect at the local DMV office to get all the information on the person, pulled up who the car belongs to. I got an address so now I'm waiting for Ken to get here so we can go run through that bitch.

"You want me to keep going daddy?"

"What do you think? Have my kids yet slid down your throat yet?

"Yeah"

 "That's what I thought!"

I put my hands on the back of her head and stood up at the same time to fuck her mouth and having all the control which is what at the time I needed.

"Yeah just like that, oh shit damn your mouth feels so good." I said as I pushed all 11 inches of my dick down her throat and sent all of my babies sliding down by water. When I got a hold of myself I shook my dick off in her mouth like I did when I took a piss in the morning and put my dick back up. "You can go now and they will escort you off of the property." I never even looked at her while she was still on her knees.

"That's it Lamar I thought we was going to fuck! And I was at least going to get paid for sucking your little dick." She yelled at me as I froze in the middle of me walking out.

"Oh, you want to get paid all right how much you want? How much do you think your mouth is worth? Huh trick." I walked over to my desk and grabbed my 45 lock I had just bought this one and it had just got delivered today I had my kids name engraved on it so since she felt some type of way I let my missing kids do the fucking talking for me. I walked back over to the girl with money in one hand and my gun in the other hand. "So, you wanna get paid lil mama? which one you want? Huh and make sure you pick the right one!"

"Lamar please don't I just thought I would get paid

because you normally throw out the girls a little cash on the side that's all but I can go now."

"Oh, no you wanted to get paid and since you serviced me with your mouth ill make the payment there as well so be a big girl and open up your mouth please like you just was for this small dick." I watch her open up her mouth with tears rolling down her face as she shook with fear my dick was getting hard just watching this shit. I shoved the money in her bra and my forty-five in her mouth as I pulled the trigger right afterwards.

"Damn bro you didn't have to do her like that." I turned around to see Ken standing in the doorway looking like I just lost my damn mind.

"So, look I got a lead on where the kids might be at we need to go check that shit out oh and call the black team to clean this shit up." I said as I grabbed the rest of my things off of my desk.

"Man, you have officially lost your damn mind we need to hurry up and find the twins so you can go on vacation or something cause this shit is not normal do you realize that the black team is going to have to chop that bitch up my nigga you nut is in her body and down her throat at that. Remember never leave a trace or have you forgot that. You haven't made a mistake so far so brody don't start now."

"Well if your done Ken can we go and honestly I could really care less or give two fucks about making a mistake as long as it leads me to my kids. So, can we go or not!"

I pushed passed his ass and walked off in the direction to his car I gave him the address and took a seat in the passenger side of the car while I sparked up a fat pre-rolled blunt. I needed to get my mind right and off of a few things too much was going on Anna and Jenn was fighting or have words. I should say, Jenn has left this dumb ass nigga and most of all my kids are still missing. This wack ass nigga Josh is nowhere to be found, I have reached out to all my connects and unless this nigga is paying people to keep his locations a secret then this nigga is really laid low because there is no reason n as to why I haven't been able to find his ass in the same fucking city. And I won't sleep until I find them I didn't even realize that the car had stop moving until this nigga Ken yelled my named.

"Lamar…. Lamar, you hear me calling nigga!"

"Yeah! I hear you nigga we here or something what nigga?"

"Yeah, we are why you over there in fucking Lala-land, what the fuck you over there thinking about anyway?"

"You sound like a bitch right now my nigga we need to hurry up and get Jenn back hell. And you already know I don't feel like talking! I feel like killing! Any and everything that is in this house! So, I'll take the front door and you take the back door. And if someone tries to leave this house kill they ass expect that bitch and Josh got it."

I hoped out the car and went to the front I knew I had lost my mind yall because it was in the middle of the damn day and I didn't give one fuck as I approached the front door and waited until I knew Ken was in the back I was about to lose no one coming out this house and for this nigga to know me he is really dumb there is no cameras on this house and no protection on his bitch he had to know I was coming for his head and hers. Once I knew Ken was in the back I covered the peep hole and knocked on the door or more like banged on the door like I was the fucking feds. It felt as if I was waiting forever at that damn door, I could hear someone moving around so I started banging even harder on that bitch.

"Yeah who the fuck is it? And why the hell are you banging on my damn door?"

I'm assuming it was the chick from the hospital because of her voice and her yanking the door open.

"Surprise bitch! Step back inside the house slowly and I swear if you try to run I'll kill you right here in the open so make your next move your best move." I said as she backed up slowly in the house she lived in a two-story town house the bitch barley had any furniture in it I swear these bad bitches yall niggas love to have, be living like bumbs for real.

"So, where is that nigga josh at?" I asked

"I don't know please don't kill me I don't have anything to do with this I've been telling him to give your kids back I don't want they crybaby asses no way!"

I slapped the bitch as soon as that statement left her mouth now don't get me wrong I usually don't hit hoes but this hoe deserved everything I was about to give her.

"Really! Do you think it's a good idea to talk shit about my kids while I'm holding a gun to your fucking temple and it don't seem like my kids are the only cry baby ones around this nasty ass house hoe? Now where is that nigga josh?"

"I swear I don't know when he left here a few hours ago he was talking about finding a way to get money from you and hitting up your traps or something I swear that's all I know but your kids are upstairs you can have they asses back."

"Bitch!" I slapped that hoe down to her knees to let her know to keep my Twins out of her scum bucket ass mouth. I see ken coming from the back. "Yo brody she said that nigga is about to try to hit the traps so make that call and have everybody on standby" I said while heading up the stairs to find my kids in this nasty ass house.

"I got you bro" ken said

I started to hear my kids crying as I approached the second floor I just needed to find what room they were in. The carpet was a dirty ass brown the walls were no longer white and it smelled like strong piss in here; I felt chills all over my body and I went cold it felt as if I could feel my kids as I walked down this pissy smelling ass hallway. Once I got to the bathroom and seen my kids in the fucking tub just lying there helpless. I had to stop myself from breaking down and crying. I picked up both of them and sat there on the edge of the tub just looking at them in awwwww my kids have gotten so big and I couldn't believe I have them back in my life.

"Yo Ken come up here really quick I'm in the bathroom and hurry up my nigga" I yelled out for him to come up here

"You got the kids?" I heard ken yelling as he ran up the stairs.

"Yeah I got them call Anna to come get our kids and have that bitch keep calling that nigga josh so we can have both of them." I said

"Yeah I got you and damn the twins have gotten so damn big man damn Mar." I watch Ken leave out the bathroom and run back down the stairs.

I wasn't leaving the bathroom until my wife got there our kids looked exactly like Anna and me a good mixture of the both of us. I couldn't believe we had them back it seemed like I was sitting I this bathroom forever. The walls were pink and it smelled like no one in life have ever cleaned this bitch, the tub had a ring that looked like black paint going around the tub there were dirty diapers all over the place and the sink looked like it didn't work either and I was getting pissed all over again until I heard Anna voice.

I swear my wife had the ability to calm me down with just one word. "Lamar baby where you at honey?" Anna called out

"I'm in here in the bathroom last door on the left?" as I yelled out for her to know which room I was in.

I watched Anna freeze in here steps at the door of the bathroom. I quickly got up with both our kids in my hands and walked over to Anna gave her a kiss on her forehead.

"Look baby I need you take the kids, go home okay? Yes! I do mean straight home okay, don't call no one, don't stop for shit matter of fact turn your phone off. Do not turn it back on until you get home… just take the kids and go home. Oh, and take the back streets… make when you get home order us some dinner okay do exactly as I'm telling you."

I watched my wife cry and hold our babies. It broke me down as a man that I couldn't protect her from this hurt and pain, that I am seeing on her face right now. Killing josh and his bitch would make me feel a lil better. I walked down the stairs behind Anna and helped her put the twins in the car and strapped them in. I had men all around this block by now so I wasn't worried about being out of this house and that nigga pulling up. Looking out for nosey ass neighbors and any cops that just might wanna play captain save a hoe today. But I was getting excited for this kill my blood started to warm up, my heart beat started to slow down, and it seemed like everything was in slow motion.

"Look Anna go straight home okay I love you and I'll see you soon okay Ma" I said to Anna as she was getting in the car

"I love you too and thank you for getting our kids back Lamar and I'm sorry for not being by your side the way I should have. But I want you to come home tonight to us okay… Lamar?"

"I'm coming…I promise" I said as I closed the car door

so she could drive off and be headed back into the house.

I closed the door and headed for the living room where the bitch was still laying on the floor crying.

"So, what's the word bro?" I asked Ken

"Well I guess the nigga was already on his way here and seen the team around in cars and tried to make a run for it but my new lil niggas I had just put on caught up with him and put that nigga in the trunk a took him to the warehouse and they are there waiting on us to get back with her."

"Alright bet well let's go then and have them burn this bitch down but I want anything that have to do with my kids and all laptops and shit out this house first and bring it to the warehouse but everything else burnt that shit."

We put her in a black sheet and carried her out to the

trunk of one of the worker's cars out the back door and made a dash to the car that was still parked down the street. We left a car parked at the house just to watch it until tonight and we made our way to the warehouse to deal with this shit.

"Hey bro do you think we should wait to handle this shit until tomorrow and you can just go home and see the kids" Ken said while driving and hoping on the freeway.

"Are you serious right now Ken now don't get me wrong I wanna go home and see and spend my time with my kids but I wanna kill them even more bro" I said lighting up another blunt.

"I hear you but damn that nigga was your bro just like I am Mar and it's just a done deal?" ken asked

"Ok look I understand how YOU feel but I loved the

nigga the same way I love you but that nigga took my kids and that is a line that you just don't cross why don't you put yourself in my shoes and what would you do? Yeah that's what I thought if I would have done that shit to either one of yall I would expect yall to do the same thing so miss me with that shit"

"Alright I hear you." Ken said turning up the music letting the shit go.

Once we made it to the warehouse I had the shop come and pick up Ken car and drop off new one so they can chop that shit down into pieces. I covered all my tracks which is why they call me a ghost cause its damn near like I was never there, I made sure of that I texted Anna to make sure she was okay and everything went smooth. Once I stepped in the room where they had them at I felt my body get cold and I zoned out to the point where I didn't even realize that I shot that nigga Josh in the knees already.

"Yo my nigga you good we couldn't even get in here or be in here a good ten fucking min damn and you shooting niggas already in the knees and shit." Ken tapping my arm to try to get me to snap out of it.

I know what I'm about to say is going to sound crazy but I was about to treat these two like a full 3 course meal and enjoy that shit too.

"You already know what it is bro." I said to ken as I pulled up a chair to sit in front of Josh.

"So, can you tell me why my nigga why did you take my kids Josh?" I asked as calmly as I could at the moment.

"Because you have always taken what was mine nigga! My spot! my money! my bitches! Nigga everything and I want that top spot so yeah I took your fucking kids so what and I drugged your bitch I hope your fucking world come crashing down all around you!" Josh yelled while bleeding out from the knees.

"Well let me tell you this you fucked with the wrong one and you of all people should know that you watched me become the man I am today and as far as your money my nigga you had that you just wanted more than you was willing to work for and your spot that's laughable my nigga we all know the big homie was going to give it to me or Ken I never thought it would be me but now Ken has that shit and as far as your bitch they were all up for grabs my nigga you tossed them around like white on rice and you fucked over a good one and that was my sister my nigga you could have had it all but you had to be greedy. So now since you wanted to see who I really am and since you thought it was cool to touch what was mine it's your turn. You love that bitch over there? Huh well I can see it in your eyes that you do but don't worry I'm not going to touch her ass I have a wife at home but I think Ken got a few niggas that might wanna run up in that thang before I off her ass. Aye Ken go downstairs and get a few new niggas and tell them we have some pussy up here for them." I yelled out over my shoulder never taking my eyes off of Josh seeing the tears up in the corner of his eyes.

I got up out the chair I was sitting in and tied that nigga up in the chair. I heard the niggas coming in the room and I got excited.

"Well it looks like the party is about to begin, now I don't need to watch cause I'm about to go home and fuck my wife so have a good night watching your bitch get fucked in about every whole." I said as I sent two shots in his shoulders and headed for the door to make my exit with Ken on my heels.

"Tell them to keep that nigga alive as much as they can I don't want him to die just yet." I said to Ken as I got in the car for him to take me back home to my family.

"Alright I got you, let me take your crazy as home man my sis need to do something with your crazy ass because I think you have officially lost your mind today".

"Well hopefully now my life can get back on track now that I have found them and I got my kids back but enough about me tho, what are you going to do about my fucking sis Jenn?"

"Well I'm going to ask her to marry me if I have you and Anna blessing all I need to do is find out where she took her ass too and get her back to Atlanta now."

"Well good luck on getting Anna blessing but you have min all day long on marrying the sis I'm glad you are growing up and doing right by her. We have had more bitches than one man is allowed to have so it's only right that we settle down now."

"Yeah I hear your bro I do and I'm going to get this shit right with Jenn no matter what. But look let's go in this house and see the kids and let me talk to sis."

"Alright bet hell I didn't even realize that we were here I must be high as hell bro." damn what a day I have had I'm just so ready to go and lay down……

Chapter 9 Anna

So here I am sitting in my room in my big bed with my twins, I've missed so much of their lives. They are now three months and so damn big yall Lamar junior looks just like his father and little Lela was a lil cry baby. I can see this is going to have to get broke cause I'm not dealing with this shit all she wanted was to be held and I can't just hold her all the time I don't know what she thinks this is.

I couldn't wait till Lamar got here so he can spend time with his kids. I knew he was going to be spending time at the warehouse for a min tonight and deal with whoever he found at that house. I just hope he get done quick.

I sent Jenn a text message letting her know that we have the kids back and that her god kids would love to see her. We still haven't been spoken since our meet up. I wish I would have known that she felt some type of way about me or our relationship that we have. I never wanted her to feel like she was living in my shadow but I hope she come back to Atlanta soon.

I knew she was living or in L.A because Mom and Ketta had texted me when she had landed and they had picked her up from the airport. I had already called Mom and Ketta and they are already on their way back to Atlanta. I got an ear full from mom that I'm passing on to Lamar since he wanted to be the one to send her out to California not me.

My baby girl crying got me out of my own thoughts so I

guess it's time to feed lil mama. "You're a hungry mama's girl alright let's go downstairs and make your bottle while your brother is sleep."

Junior laid on the bed sleep like a grown man like he had just got in from work or something. I guess he learned how to self sooth because he was out like a light. Chill just like his damn daddy.

I got up and headed down to the kitchen to make her bottle so I can feel lil mama. I heard the front door chime so I knew Lamar was home and I knew he had Ken right along with his ass. Most of the time if you see Lamar then you see Ken ass as well. I swear them two never went nowhere without the other. "Lamar I'm in the kitchen." I yelled out so he could hear me.

"What are you in here doing? And what is my baby doing? And why is she crying like that?" Lamar asked walking up on me taking his daughter out my arms.

"Well I'm in here making her a bottle first off, and you baby is being a spoiled lil brat, and I have no idea why she is crying like this Lamar you do know I'm knew to this so don't start with me." I said taking the bottle out of the microwave and putting the milk in it before I handed it to Lamar so he can feed his baby.

"Hey why didn't you make the bottle in the room Anna that's why I had the kitchen put in there so we won't have to come down here and make them. And where is Junior at?"

I swear yall this man had so much to fucking say he was starting to work my damn nerve. "Well I forgot the kitchen was up there and Junior is in the room asleep in the middle of our bed like a grown ass man I swear he reminds me of you. Oh, we need to take them to the doctor in the morning and to the mall to get their ears pierced. But I really think now that we have the kids back bae we should really have a family dinner but mom and Ketta and Jenn has to be here and that's a must." I turned to look at Ken who was sitting at the island looking at his phone waiting for it to ring or something I walked over to him and took a seat next to him.

"Look ken I know you love my sister but I swear if you don't fix this shit between yall I will fuck you up myself and play with me if you want to" I said looking him dead in his eyes

"Well that is what I wanted to talk to you about Lil Sis." Ken said looking up from his phone finally.

"Okay I'm listening" I said waiting to hear what he had to say.

"well I talked to big bro on the way here but I told him I wanted to ask you as well, I wanna marry your sister Anna and I wanted to asked you if it's cool with you." Ken asked looking like he was holding his damn breath

"Of course, you can marry my sister and have you delete all your hoes yet out that phone you holding on tight too because I can tell you that is something she will be looking for." I said getting up and giving him a hug while heading up stairs.

"Lamar I'm heading upstairs to get some rest I'm guessing I'll be seeing you up here soon ken you don't have to go home but you have to get the hell out of here no matter of fact you do have to go home." I made sure to put a lil extra in my walk because I knew he as was watching me walk away.

I haven't felt my man in so long it was about damn time

and tonight was going to be the night. I stepped in the room to see my baby boy layed out on the bed still sleep. I just had to take a look at him he had curly hair a Carmel skin tone to him light hazel eyes and was Hella long. He was a little chunk little man when he was born but he had slimmed out.

I picked him up off of the bed and walked him to his room and put him in his crib. I pressed play on the wall monitor to turn on the baby music and turned it down so it wouldn't wake him up. As I was walking out the room I cracked the door and I heard Lamar saying his good byes to Ken so I knew he was going to be on his way upstairs soon.

I went back in our room and started to clean off our bed I had so much stuff on it that it didn't make any damn sense. Since I didn't know what I needed so I had everything in this damn bed. I put everything back in the containers I had took them out of and placed them back in the corner by the door to take them back out of the room in the morning.

When I was done with that I had made my way into the bathroom to start my shower I didn't feel like sitting in a hot ass tub of water I needed it to fall around me and all over my head since we had the three-sixty showers I was able to really enjoy it. I turned on my Pandora on my favorite station and let my music take me away to another place.

I stepped out of my clothes and stepped in the shower and when I felt that water hit my skin and I was in heaven. I heard Lamar entering the bathroom trying to sing along with song by TGT-I need you. "Lamar don't kill my vibe trying to sing." I said while laughing at his silly ass "where is my daughter at by the way?" I asked.

"Well if you must know she is sleeping next to her brother she seemed to be more comfortable that way instead of sleeping alone." Lamar said

"Well stop talking and get in here already if you getting in!" I said while sticking my head under the water to let it fall over my head. I felt the cold air hit my ass before I felt Lamar behind me wrapping his hands around my waist as Keke Wyatt song falling in love started to play sending chills through my body even in a hot shower my body still went cold at his touch.

"I've missed you Anna." My husband said as he kissed me on the back of my neck while letting his hands slide right to my honey pot and wrapped his other hand around my neck to keep me in place.

And took me on my first ride for the night as my body shock as I got my first orgasm.

"Tell me what you want Anna, tell me what you want me to do to you Anna?"

"Make love to me Lamar." I said damn near in tears as Lamar turned me around and backed me against the tile as he kissed me. As his lips parted mine and his tongue found mine I could taste the weed on his tongue that mixed in with his sweetness. As Lamar lifted me up like I weighed little to nothing putting my legs on his shoulders as my back was against the wall as he went in to eat my pussy like it was his last meal. I swear this man had the gift to eat the soul out of me. I couldn't deal with that much pleasure this high up I mean damn this nigga was 6'4 so I was up to high to have this much pleasure happening to me at the moment.

"Lamar baby I can't deal baby damn baby! Ohhhh shit! Yeah right there! I'm Cumming! Lamar yeah got dammit daddy!" As I was coming down off of that roller-coaster he slides me down his body wrapping my legs back around his waist as he slides his dick into me inch by inch filling me up to the point where I felt as if I didn't have any room left in me; as he played and kissed on my breast as he keeps me still.

"Baby wine them hips for Daddy let me feel that shyt baby." Lamar said in my ear as he kissed all on my neck. I did as I was told that's one thing I could do is wine my hips. So, I started off slow since I haven't felt this man in so long it all felt so new to me.

"Come on ma put that shit on me!" Once again, I did as I was told I wined my hips in a circle motion. As he matched my movements as the water was dripping from our skin. All you heard was both of us moaning and our skin smacking together as Lamar picked up his speed bringing me out my thoughts.

"Ma I'm about to nut, I want you to bust with me shit you feel too damn good. But I'm not done with you yet"

He carried me from the shower to our bedroom still dripping wet and laid me on the bed. I just layed across the bed just looking at his body got my pussy wet all over again.

"Now is it my turn daddy" I asked as I sat up while Lamar was looking at me.

"Yea it's your turn show me what you got lil mama"

I slide off the bed to give my man this deep throat he's been missing as I wrapped my lips around the tip of his dick and slowly made my way all the way down taking all of him in with ease. Tickling the back of my throat with the head of his dick then getting sloppy with it just how I knew he liked it. It sounded like I was slurping on a big stick ice cream by the way this shit sounded.

"Damn ma!"

I heard Lamar say as I was about to take him to the edge of no return. I cupped his balls in one hand, sucked and licked with my mouth, and just as I pushed him down my throat I felt his seeds slide down it.

"Bend that ass over Ma right now! I'm done playing with you tonight"

"Yes sir" I said as I climb back up on our bed and tooted my ass in the air. Just like he liked it. He then ran his fingertips down the center of my back to give me an even deeper arch than the one I have. He slid his dick in me so nice and slow he knew that shit drove me crazy, as he sped up I felt his thumb slide in my ass.

That took things to a whole different level and he knew I loved that nasty shit.

"Play with your pussy Ma and throw that ass back!"

I reached down under me and to play with my clit like I was told. "Ohhhh! Damn baby this yo pussy daddy take this shit!"

"I swear Anna if you ever give this shit away again I will kill you with my bare hands you hear me? This is my pussy it got my name all over it you hear me!"

"Yes! Daddy yes! I hear you now, harder, harder Lamar yes daddy!" I felt his dick getting thicker than it already was, so I knew he was on the verge of nutting. So, I squeezed my pussy tight around his dick.

And I knew he could feel that shit cause just as I was on my wave of cumming and he did too. Falling out on the side of the bed beside me. "Ma I swear I think I just put twins back in you, so be prepared to be knocked up again really soon if I keep giving you this dick like this.

I heard Lamar laughing like that shyt was funny or something. "I bet not be you is tripping." I looked over at Lamar and see that that nigga was knocked out. "Yea my pussy is Nyquil in this bitch" I said laughing to myself as I pull our throw cover on top of us.

Just as I was about to close my eyes I heard the twins start to cry I looked over at the clock and it was almost three in the damn morning. Well at least I had some alone time and some dick before they woke up. I looked over to tell Lamar to get his ass up to help me but this nigga was snoring like he was in a field all day working. But I guess this is the first night that he has had a good night sleep. So, I slipped out the bed and put on a robe to go attend to my kid's solo bolo tonight I guess......

Chapter 10 Jenn

Soo...... I made it to L.A four in a half hours later with Ketta picking me up. It's been a week since I've been here and can honestly say I'm ready to go back home. But I need my space, and my time from Ken. I know that if I'm in the same city then that is not going to happen. Anna texted me the other day to let me know that they had found the kids she also sent me some pictures and I can say that they have gotten so damn big now.

I had order them some clothes and stuff and had it sent to the house for them. Even through I'm not there don't man that my god mother's duties are out the window. I love them kids like they came out my pum-pum. That is why I'm torn that I'm not there I gave her so much hell about being there and look at me.

But hey I have my reason's I guess, I'm being selfish cause I need a clear head. Ketta and mom had left two days after, I got here once they got word that the kids were back, but I don't think they really planning on coming back. I heard my phone going off to let me know that the lift driver was here at the hotel I was going to be staying at.

I grabbed my gym bag, my purse, and made my way out the hotel. I needed to work out and get a lil more tone to my body. Then I was going to meet with a realtor to look at a few houses for the boys and girl's houses.

I had only had one requirement and they had to be side

by side and that I could do work on them. I had enlisted the bad ass Sontigo sister from Miami, you can check them out in sleeping with the plugs daughter by Mo Houston. Any who, they had the hottest houses. Nichole was having her assistant flying in to meet me and show me a few.

Twenty minutes later I was pulling in front of the gym, making sure my driver had got paid from my phone account. All this shit is new to me I could have just drove, but I was about to get lost in this big ass city, so hell naw not me… I don't do well lost.

I walked in the twenty-four-hour fitness gym to check in with my trainer Shawn for the day, she came highly recommend, and when I tell yall her body was so on point so I knew she wasn't no joke.

"You ready to work and get into it." I heard her say from

behind me by the locker room door. I turned around seeing my trainer with her in shape ass body.

"Now look I'm not here trying to get my body like yours at all." I said as I watched her face frown up.

"So, what the fuck you doing here then because what I don't do is waste time or got time to be playing with you. So, either we are going to work out the way I want to or you can take your ass home." I looked at her like she had lost her damn mind, but I could get with it tho.

"Alright then let's get to it because I have a few places to go afterwards." I said walking into the locker room to put my stuff up.

I can't lie to yall not two fucking hours later my whole body was sweating in places where I have never in my whole life before, hell not even during sex with Ken; so, he was slacking. "Well Miss Shawn thank you very much and if I choose to stay in L.A I'll be back."

"Alright well I'll be looking forward to seeing you again." I grabbed my phone, I had seen I had a few miss calls from Anna & Ken, but I wasn't ready to speak to either one of them. Seen I had a text message from my realtor as well, with the address to meet him at so we can go, and look at these houses.

I grabbed my pink tote bag with my change of clothes in it and headed for the showers. Once I got showered and changed I checked to see if my lift driver was out front as I made my way in that direction.

Once I was in the car and on my way my phone going off in my bag caught my attention because my mind was in the freaking clouds. I see Ken name flashing across my screen one person I didn't feel like speaking too at all or dealing with. But my heart was telling me to answer because I wanted to hear his voice.

"Hello Ken" I said with a little too much attitude in my voice that I hope he was ready for.

"So now your childish self-have time to answer the phone for me?"

"I swear Kenndrick if you wanna talk then talk, but don't start that shyt with me. I picked up the phone. So, say what the fuck you got to say!" I said while looking out the window waiting to hear a response… so speak damn!

"Look Ma" Ken said as I interrupted his ass

"My name is not no fucking Ma its either Jenn or Jennifer, but I need you to choose one"

"Well Jennifer, Jenn or whatever the fuck your name is at the moment. You wanna be fucking called you need to come home, so we can talk and fix this shit. I want my woman back and I need you back in my life Jenn and I think you already know that. But what do I have to do to prove this shit to you huh Jenn?"

"Are you done yet?" I said not giving two fucks about all that bullshit he just said

"Well if you are listing right now listen up really good because I'm only going to say this shit once. I want a man that knows how to keep his dick that should only belong to me and me only in his fucking pants! And knows how to respect me when I'm in and out of his presence. In this relationship, I want a man that's knows what being faithful means. That's what I want Ken. You may be the king of them streets you out there in, but just know this I can take care of my damn self. And I don't need you to do shit for me. That's what you need to realize so if you want to be the king of this relationship and have me treat you like the king you are then you need to start treating me like the QUEEN I am! And by the way I have some movers coming by to move the rest of my things out of your house. And I swear for the life of me I don't want any issues Ken. If you want this woman back and I do mean WOMAN, you have some work to put in. Before I come back to you."

"Okay all that is cool and all, but yeah I heard you Jenn I did… And what the fuck you mean you got some movers and people coming to my house to move your shit? Now let me tell you something which I think you already know. No one is coming in my better yet OUR fucking house to move a got damn thing! And if you wanna try me you can have a few dead bodies on your hands. Because I will kill every last one of them, and since you say you know me. then you should know I'm not fucking around with you right now. So, if you want your shit then you are more than welcome to try and come get it your damn self. And before you even think about it NOBODY! Is walking in our house taking shit no mommy's, sisters, brothers, cousins, NOBODY Jenn! So, I guess I'll be seeing you sooner than I thought if you want your shit doll face oh my bad I mean Jenn." Ken said hanging up the phone.

I can't believe I'm about to have to go back all the fucking way to Atlanta just to deal with this nigga. And just when I needed space this nigga here pull this shyt. Yall reading this that is one thing that nigga Ken could do is figure out a way to pull you back in to his bullshit.

I noticed we were pulling up to a house that I was supposed to be looking at and I really wasn't feeling it at all. So, I informed the driver just to take me back to the hotel. I sent the guy an email letting him know something had come up. I also sent Nichole an email informing her to just send me the details of the house that best fit my needs and I will make a decision from there.

When I was done with that I went to southwest online and booked me a flight back home that was leaving tonight. So, I had enough time to go get packed and get some good food while I waited at the airport. I'm just mad I didn't have enough time to go shopping while I was here. And this nigga Ken will be giving me my money back for that damn flight.

I made note to call his mom Miss Yolanda to talk to her she lives in Oakland, CA so we didn't get a chance to see her as often as Lamar mom but we keep in contact. And I need her words of wisdom right about now. Because I just didn't understand this Man at all.

Once I made it to my room I sent Anna a text message letting her know that I would be back tomorrow and I'll be stopping by so we can figure this stuff out. I asked mom or Ketta to pick me up since I didn't have my car still at the airport I had it picked up and towed back to my house from the airport.

Once all that was did, and I arrived back at the hotel I packed all my shit and made my way to the airport to go back to fucking Atlanta the home of the fucking love… I just pray Ken aint with the shit when I get there but who am I fooling this is Ken we are speaking of.

I stopped at a nearby restaurant called Angeline's Louisiana Kitchen and grab me some food. I order so much food I wish I could take It back with me but I had an hour to get to the airport and check it and I didn't plan on missing my flight. I was able to pick out two house

that I needed to run by Ketta and Jenn to see what they

thought and then we could go from there.

Chapter 11 Ken

 So look yall know what's going on between Jenn and

me. Hell Jenn left my ass and went to L.A she tried to tell

me that some movers were coming in my house to get her

shit but you know I wasn't having that shit. My mom

called me and told me they talked and told me she was

picking her up from the airport.

So I had come up with a plan and I had to beg mom's to

go along with the shit. But once I got mom's on board to

go along with it. I had my styles pick out a bad as dress

for Jenn to put on at her hotel. I had jewelry, shoes, a hair and makeup girl there at her hotel even through my bitch didn't need nor wear makeup like that but I Knew she liked that shit.

I had edible arrangements delivered to her room I also had white roses everywhere. When I say, I was going to get my bitch I mean my woman I need to stop referring to her as my bitch tho on some real shit. But any fucking way I had changed her room to the penthouse at the Marriott I had a car ready to pick her up when she was finally ready with all this unnecessary ass shit.

So if yall haven't figured it out yet I'm about to ask Jenn to be my wife and I hope she says yes. And yes, I know it's only been a week since all that shit ween down but hey a guy can hope right. I mean look at everything Lamar and Anna been through and if they can make it hell me and Jenn could.

I've went through too much shit for her not to say yes. I had this place deck out with flowers too and shit all over my floors. With chefs in my kitchen cooking up her favorite foods.

I even had Dondre ready to sing you're the one as soon as she walked in the door. I was about to get my lady back by any means necessary. Because I'm not waking up another day without her. I needed to go meet up with Lamar at the jewelry store to pick up the ring.

I know I waited to the last minute to get it but hell this was the only time I could pull him away from his wife and kids. And who better to have with me hell Anna wasn't really feeling me until I make shit right with Jenn. And I really don't blame her, so even though they got their issues they were still rocking hard for one another.

"Aye look yall I'm about to make a run before this shit happen in a few hours. If yall fuck this shit up or my house just know I'll kill all of yall. So, don't go looking around because I do have camera and don't think about stealing shit. I'm leaving Dondre in charge so get this shit right." I said as I grabbed my keys off the table in the living room.

"Hey D I'm about to go pick up the ring if you need to change I have a room for you down the hall and call me if anything happens. I shouldn't be gone too long it's not that far."

"Alright Ken I got you I'll see you back here soon." Dondria said walking off.

I hopped in my car and headed to the jewelry office. I can't believe I'm about to make it official and ask this woman to be my wife. I just be crazy if this is what I'm about to do man. I said to no one since I was in this damn car alone. I quickly got off the freeway on my exit that I was about to pass because I was sitting here in my damn feelings and shit taking me off my square.

I pulled up parking next to this nigga big ass Hummer I swear this nigga get a different car every week. This nigga could own a fucking dealership with all the cars he has that is a damn shame.

"Nigga if you get one more fucking car I'm stealing that shit." I said while laughing at that nigga.

"Yea I see you laughing now but you won't be laughing after you put that ring on my sis finger tho man, you will be buying stupid ass shit thinking that will make up for lil shit. Like not putting the toilet seat down among Hella other bullshit. But look before you go in here are you sure you wanna do this? Are you sure you wanna put a ring on it?" Lamar asked me

"I'm as sure as this hundred K I got in my pocket for this damn ring I'm about to put on her finger. But man, I can't live without that woman. I don't even know why we still standing out here talking."

"We are out here because I wanna make sure you know what you are getting and signing up for. That's my lil sis now and I'm not about to let you hurt her at all or again. So, I'm going to ask you this one more time are you sure you wanna do this?" Lamar said this time adding a little more bass in his voice.

I must have looked at this nigga like he was crazy.

"Man if you don't move your corny big brother ass out my way I'm on a timeline and I don't have all day to be sitting out here talking to you about this shit." I pulled out a pocket full of money and just looked at him like can we go in now or what.

"Alright let's go do this then." Lamar said walking in the building

Two fucking hours later and all my money I brought with me and then some I walked out of there with an Auriga eighteen-k two-toned gold twenty-two one and half TDW certified Yellow Diamond Halo ring. Yall if she says no to this ring and me I'm bring this bitch back and getting me a chain and think I'm playing. I went all out I bet yall wished yall no good ass niggas went out like I did huh? Ha-ha but its only one Ken me and Mar said our good byes and I told the nigga I'll get at him a lil later.

I headed back to the house to start getting ready for the big night. I got a text from my mom saying that she just dropped Jenn off at the hotel and it was almost go time. I got a text message from Jenn as well.

Jenn: I don't know what you are up too but I'm so not falling for this corny ass shit, but thank you for the gifs. And I guess I'll be seeing you soon.

I just looked at the message and shook my head I swear she try to be so damn hard at times. So, I put petal to the metal or however you say that corny ass shit. Once I made it back home yall I swear once I walked in the house ill marry my damn self just by the looks of this shyt. I had so many damn roses in here in every damn room in every damn color all over my fucking house. I swear you only see shit like this in movies.

If I was able to pull this off yeah, I'm that nigga yall love to hate. I went up to my room to start getting ready. I had my suite layed out on the bed with the shoes and shit to match yea I was putting it all together. Once I hopped out the shower and got my swag on I looked myself over and I must say your boy was killing it. I sent Jenn a quick message

Ken: I am truly sorry for how I acted I'm just asking that you come into tonight with an open mind and heart I love you baby see you soon.

I'm hoping she be cool yall, you never know who you are going to get with her. So now I'm just waiting I went downstairs to make sure everything was ready. The food was done and had the house smelling Hella good. I had the chef cooking all seafood I mean dips and crab cakes pasta and a bunch of other shit. Since I knew she loved that shit so now I'm sitting in the living room waiting for her driver to pull up.

I had GPS on the car so I knew when they left the hotel hell I could see turn by turn. I had Dondria waiting by the front entrance so she could start singing as soon as the door opened. I checked the phone and seen she was about to pull down the street.

"Alright yall she about to be here in few seconds don't fuck this up." I yelled as I stood up to go stand by Dondria……

"Okay Dondria don't let me down sing like you never sang before." I said looking at her and then back at the door.

"I was born ready let's get you engaged so I can get the hell up out of this house with your crazy ass."

I could hear the door closes and her footsteps getting closer and closer. As soon as the door opened…… Dondria let the music flow

I don't believe that we were put together not to be together

And I don't believe there's anyone out there that can love me better

I don't believe that you know how much I miss seeing your pretty smile

Of course, we had our ups and downs

But I gotta have you around me cause

I feel it all over my body

I dream about you when I sleep (yea)

You're the one for me (you're the one)

You're the one for me (you're the one)

All the signs say that

Ever since the day that we laid eyes on each other baby

You're the one for me (you're the one)

You're the one for me (hey)

I don't believe that you know how much I melt when I smell your sent girl

And I don't believe I got myself in this predicament

I'm sorry (I'm so sorry)

For everything I ever did girl

I'm sorry (I'm so sorry)

And I'm begging you, begging you, begging you, begging you please come back home.

When I lay in our bed at night

I'm hoping and praying that you feel the same way I do deep down inside

And that feeling you just can't control

It makes you wanna just call me

And tell me how much you really miss me

It makes you wanna call me

And say that you can't wait to hold and kiss me, kiss me all over.

I watched my girl walk in the house with a look I wish I could get a picture of I seen the tears rolling down her face. But she looked so damn good. In her all red vera Wang dress. That cost me a fucking grip.

"Ken what are you up too and why is Dondria here singing one of my favorite songs?"

"Baby just come in and let me explain what is going on right now please just let me talk okay" I said as Dondria switch songs over to Anthony Hamilton The Point of It All.

"I know vie fucked up and I know you may think I'm full of shit but one thing I know for sure is that I'm supposed to spend the rest of my life with you. Now I know you may think I'm just saying this because you let but trust me when I say this I would do everything in my power for you right now at this moment."

"What are you saying Ken" Jenn said wiping her tears away

"Maybe I can show you" as I got down on my knee I watched her eyes get big.

"I'm saying or better yet I'm asking you Jennifer will

you be my wife, my rider, my forever, my better half. Through all the bullshit all the good times will you do me the honor knowing I don't deserve you but will you be my wife."

"Yes! Yes! Yes! Kenndrick I will marry your crazy ass now get up off the floor and kiss me already." Jenn said pulling me up after I put the ring on her finger.

"Damn ma I can't believe you said yes, wait I can call you Ma now right lol?"

"No you can call me your wife now lol, yes daddy you can call me Ma or whatever you want to with this big ass rock you just slipped on my finger."

I looked over at Dondria and gave her the look where she could make her exit I didn't need her any longer.

"Well believe it because you are mine for life now

there's no getting out of this now, well Ma lets go eat I got all of your favorite foods waiting for you." I said turning to walk towards the kitchen.

"Ken if you think I want any food any food right now after you just asked me to marry you then you got me messed up. I'm hungry alright but not for no damn food."

"Oh, is that so?" I asked looking at her while taking my suite coat off "well stay right here and don't move let me make sure the house is empty." I walked through that house so damn fast and made sure all the doors were locked and turned on the music. And made my way back in the living room where Jenn was.

Once I stepped foot back in the living room and seen my future wife standing there in nothing but her heels I knew I was in for a wild ass night. I had to grab my dick just to calm down.

"Damn Ma you are so fucking sexy ma!"

"Then why don't you come over here and show mw how sexy I am then Daddy!"

I stepped up to the plate ready to fuck the shit out of her. I picked her up and kissed the shit out of her to let her know just how much I missed her and how much I wanted her body at that moment. I layed her on the table while I took a seat in the chair.

"Ken what you doing baby? She asked looking confused

"Well you may not be hungry but I am and I'm about eat my meal so open up them legs for daddy" I said looking serious as hell. I helped her part her legs as I licked and sucked all over her clit and felt her juices run down my chin. And she tasted like sweet ass pineapple's

"Damn Ma you taste so fucking good" I said in between

sucking the shit out of her clit as she tried to close her legs "naw ma keep them open for me

"Damn Ken I'm about to cum daddy please stop baby I can't take it please Ohhhh shit baby" Jenn called out.

I stood up and unbuckled my pants and let them fall down around my ankle while I played with her clit and watcher her squirm trying to get out my hold. As I entered my dick into her so damn slow I just wanted to make love to her. So, I lifted her off the table and carried her to the room that was down the hall and layed her on the bed as I started to take my time with her.

"Ken please baby stop playing with me and fuck me we can make love another time just fuck me daddy." Jen said with so much serious in her voice that shit turned me on even more. I picked up my pace and lifted her back up and placed her back against the wall as I held her legs in the crock of my arm.

As I started to beat her shit all up………

"This my pussy Jenn?"

"Yes, daddy damn slowdown"

"Hell, naw you wanted this I wanted to make love to you and take my time but you wanted this dick hard and rough so this is what you get."

Once I felt the orgasm she let lose I was right behind her

"Damn ma why you just cum like that and make a nigga bust?"

"You did that shit daddy not me"

"Well come ride this dick then wifey!" I said as I let her down and layed on the bed waiting for her to clime this mountain that never went down.

"Anything you say baby but can I taste it first?"

"Hell, yea but I swing that ass up here don't be stingy with that sweet ass you got."

I watch her crawl on the bed and wrap her lips around my dick and I damn near bust off the warmth of mouth alone as she placed her pussy lips in my face and I went to town this was my way of still being in control because Jenn was way too damn good with her tongue and mouth for me.

I felt her starting to ride my face as she deep throated my dick and played with my nuts. I swear this woman knew exactly what to do to me.

"Damn ma Ohhhh shit ma slow down" I said all you could hear was her sucking and licking all over my shit I could barely focus on hat the fuck I had to do.

"Awwwww! Shit I'm about to bust Ma sit up Awwwww! Shit Ma" I let my load off in her mouth and she swallowed that shit which was a turn on because Jenn didn't do that shit at all.

"Damn ma really like that"

"Well you mine now so you can have all of me and I do mean all of me" Jenn said sliding down my body as she mounted me from the back riding me reverse cowgirl. As she made her ass bounce as I slapped her ass and let her do her thing.

"Yea ma work that shit so I can do what I do best." I was waiting for her to get her next orgasm once I felt her muscles tighten up on my dick so I knew it was about that time. So, I grabbed her hips and went to work.

"Kennnnnnnn! Damn! Hold up babe! Awwwww! Shit

daddy! Right their baby Ohhhh shit yes daddy I'm Cumming baby! Aww fuck Ken.

As soon as I felt her shit run down my dick I let loose in her.

"Damn ma you have worn me the fuck out"

"Well I'm not done yet let's go get et this food baby and then we can pick back up in the shower upstairs"

I just look at her like she had lost her mind as she hopped up off my dick and walked out her room towards the kitchen yelling I'm his wifey now bitches. What the fuck have I gotten myself into yall. I hopped up off the bed and grabbed my boxers and went towards the kitchen when I heard her singing along with the music that was playing through the house on the sound system.

I leaned against the wall as I watch her dance to the

music and eat the now cold ass food but she didn't give

two fucks at all

"I love you Jenn and thank for being my wife." I said as

she turned around and walked over to me and placed the

most loving kiss on me.

Chapter 12 Lamar

Damn! Yall I got my kids back and me and Anna is doing great what more could a man ask for right now. I had to write my name back in that pussy of her's but she will understand when she finds out she is pregnant again with my kids I swear I can't wait to have a full fucking house of kids. Well its Sunday fun day with the family Jenn was back in town and we haven't heard from her nor that nigga Ken so I guess she said yeah to his dumb ass.

Mom and Ketta been back for a few days now and I must say I missed they ass and its nothing like having your mom and family around you. My mom couldn't get enough of the kid's hell Ketta didn't let them out of her sight most of the time either.

We were having dinner here at the house tonight Ken and Jen will be coming I hope. And hopeful Jen and Anna can talk that shit out and if not then mom is going to have to fix that shit. Because I really don't have the time to deal with that girly ass shit. I want us to take a family vacation soon so they need to get their shit together.

But first I still have that shit at the warehouse to wrap up it's been almost two weeks and I don't have time to keep stalling. I'm just waiting on Anna to say she ready to deal with this shit I'm learning not to do shit without her nowadays. I had got her an all-white and gold Beretta with the kid's name engraved on the side of hers like I did for mine. So she can know who the fuck we out here riding for.

"Hey bro where the fuck you at in this big ass house." I heard Ketta yelling out for me for no damn reason at all.

"I'm out here in the back yard what's good lil sis and why the fuck is you yelling trick?"

I waited to see my sis pop her big ass head out the sliding door.

"Hey me and Anna is about to go to the mall and get a few things for the kids so we should be back in an hour or so and mom is in the twin's room with them like always kk."

"What the fuck hell no, no, no fucking KK what is wrong with yall if my wife is going then I'm going too. So let me go get my shit on and we can take the hummer and be on our way." I said as I made my way towards the door

I watch Ketta step closer to me and close the door behind her.

"No Lamar look big bro I know you may be scared to lose her or whatever but she needs her space for just a min we will be back okay in an hour trust me enjoy this time with the kids or go and get some work done or something she just need some girl time that's all brody I got your wife."

I looked at my sis like she had me fucked up but I did understand where she was coming from a lil bit.

"Alight well damn at least take one of my cars so I can know yall cool and I'll see yall when you get back and take care of my wife Ketta."

"Lamar last time I checked I'm a grown ass woman and I don't need your sister to take care of me nor look out for me." Anna said steeping in the backyard.

I heard my wife say as she walked towards me and sat her thick ass on my lap.

"Now you know you can't just sit on my lap with all that ass." I whispered in her ear so only she could hear me hear me.

"Not unless you wanna go upstairs to the room or in the pool house you may wanna get your pretty ass up Ma before I have you in the room screaming out my name." I said to Anna as she had a smirk on his face

"Baby boy bye, bye come on sis lets go before I can't get his ass off of me." Anna said hoping her ass off of me

"Yeah I see yall back doing good I need the secret so I can find me a fucking man." Ketta said while turning around getting ready to walk back in the house.

"You don't need a fucking man sis and keep playing with me. Hell you see what happen with the last nigga you called yourself dating or fucking with so be single for a while and enjoy being my lil sister Ketta." I said to Ketta because she had me fucked up all the way around.

"See brody that's where you need to understand that I'm a big girl by now and when I go back to L.A you can't stop me from Atlanta so I'll let you think you will and can but trust me I'll show you. And don't judge me off of my past relationships. Hell, that was my boyfriend for a brief second but that was your boy for a lifetime remember that." Ketta said walking away.

"Yeah whatever, yall hurry up and come back." I said watching the girls leave the out the backyard. Once the girls were gone I made my way upstairs to check on my kids and found my mama in there with them.

"Hey mama you know you don't have to sit in here with the kids right."

"Boy I know but I've missed out on so much time I need to get that back by spending time so go on and do whatever you need to do I know you have work to do." My mom said shoving me out the room.

"Well alright I'll be in my office if you need me."

"We won't."

I heard my mom call out as I was making my way out the room to my office. Damn yall my life has really been changed. I can't believe I have two kids and a wife. I was just a normal nigga on the prowl for the next bitch to slide my kids down her throat. Now I'm wifed up and I'm starting to think it's time for me and the family to leave the Atlanta area and make that move to L.A.

I know my mom wants to go back but don't want to leave us. But I think that's a conversation I think I may have to have with Anna later tonight at dinner or before. I poured myself a shot of Hennessy and sat at my desk to start working on a few things.

Hell, two hours had passed and a whole bottle of Henny later I noticed that the girls hadn't returned yet. See I knew they asses were up to no good but I had no damn idea what until I checked Anna GPS system on the car to see they were about fifteen min away from the house. But I could also see they went to my damn warehouse also.

I knew exactly what she went there for so I logged into the camera system to see what had happen there. I watched Anna, Ketta and Jenn to my surprise pull into parking lot and get out of the car. I noticed Anna had changed her clothes man what the fuck was really going on with my wife.

She had on all black I mean all black hoodie she had her hair pulled back in a high ponytail. Damn she looked Hella good right now. I watched her put her hand on the scanner to get let in. after that she walked straight up into the room where we had Josh and his bitch at and pulled out her forty-five I think she had that bitch customer made because that bitch was rose gold with the matching silencer to go with it I watch her screw on.

I watched her start beating the girl ass and I mean like she had classes. Like she knew exactly what she was doing. Then started on Josh I mean while Ketta and Jenn watched. While she went back and forth between the two until finally stopped. And picked up her weapon of choice and killed both of them with a shot in between the eyes. Yea my bitch was bad I us wished I know this side of her. I watched all three of them leave the same way they came in.

I couldn't believe the shit I just watched so when I heard the front door open and close I hopped up so damn fast to see what the fuck was really going on. I watched all three of them walk back into the house laughing and shit with ken following behind them.

"Mummy so what's up did yall have a good time or what?" I asked all three of them.

They changed they clothes I'm thinking to myself when did they have time to do that shyt.

"Yeah babe we did you should of came I'm going to put my things up I got today."

If you could see the fuck ass look I had on my face right now at the moment. I was looking like I had seen a fucking ghost right now. Who the fuck was this standing in front of me. Her eyes even looked different.

"What's up brody why you over here looking like you constipated or something?" Ken asked

"Man, bro lets go to the office and talk well be ready for dinner in a second yall." I said walking back to my office while Ketta and Jenn joined Anna upstairs until it was time to go eat. But I needed another drink while I let him watch this video. Because I wasn't nearly drunk enough for this shit.

"What's going on bro spill the beans dammit"

"Man go over to the desk and press play on the video from the warehouse and have a set while you watching it too." I got me and him a drink because I knew he would be needing it.

"Mar what the fuck is this shit and when did this happen?" Ken asked as he looked up at me.

"Man that shit just happened about two fucking hours ago, they just left that bitch as you can see the time on the screen."

"But they didn't have this shit on just a min ago?"

"Yea I know that is what I am saying bro and when the fuck did my wife become a fucking gangster and do see that fucking gun she is using, where and who made that shit for her?" I said as I took a seat thinking Hella hard did my wife have a double life that I didn't know about I had so many damn questions.

"Man I don't know what the fuck is going on but we do need to get to the bottom of things." Ken said still watching the video.

"Aye Ken I was thinking about moving to Cali back to L.A with mom and Ketta what do you think about that?"

"Hell yeah I'm ready to get the fuck out this city anyway we will have to travel back and forth or find someone Hella loyal to run this shit." Ken said while looking up from the screen.

"The fuck we won't nigga we can do that shit you got trust worthily people on your team and we don't need no new people." I said while talking the last gulp of Henny that was in my cup.

"Alright bet but just no my nigga if we set up out there then it's going to be a lot." Ken said while turning off the computer and walking over to the lounge area so we could smoke this blunt before we head back upstairs to go eat.

"Well ill guess we will find out at dinner" I said while taking a pull on the blunt.

Chapter 13 Anna

So yes, as yall know I killed that bitch and Josh I did it for many reasons. One being I knew Lamar wasn't going to be able to kill his childhood friend no matter what. That's why he has been letting them sit there in that dame warehouse for this long. And I didn't want them to die at the hands of one of his many workers this shit was way too personal to me.

And the bitch well I knew he would get around to it but he was taking way to damn long for my liking. Second reason was they crossed the line and took my fucking kids. Now I don't know where Josh and his now dead ass bitch got that bright idea from. But they fucked with the wrong mother and hell that was enough reason for me.

I didn't need another one now on to the question I know all of yall got. I didn't tell my husband because hell he doesn't tell me everything. And hell, I knew he would try and stop me or try and go with me. And I know he already know I just didn't feel like speaking about that shit at the moment.

Now to the good shit yall so when I was younger my dad used to teach me how to shoot guns. And taught me how to fight my mom didn't know my dad wanted me to be able to protect myself. At all cost, Lamar or yall don't need to know that side of me. I wanna be his lady a lady at all times and I don't feel like killing and toting a gun nor fighting was a part of that. I don't want Lamar to think of feel like I wanna be some type of thug chick at all.so I keep that part of my life a secret at all times. I had more guns that I knew what to do with I had a gun fetish I loved the way they looked and felt in my hands. But I didn't need Lamar seeing that I could kill a bitch or nigga with my bare hands. Or maybe if he did know that he would trip off of me like that.

But I knew he wouldn't let me go to the mall alone so I called and made up with Jenn last night while he was in his office working. And I knew Ketta ass would be down to go along with the everything without asking. Because her ass is just as crazy as her brother she is just like me at times she has a switch if you flip that bitch its wasn't no telling what she would or could do.

Once we got back to the house and I see the look on

Lamar face I knew he knew and wanted answers. So, I was going wait after dinner to explain everything to him and take him to my storage and I'm hoping he don't flip the fuck out.

Me and the girls are sitting in my closet having drinks and talking while I put up all this shit I had Ketta go to the mall and buy yesterday.

"So when do you think you are going to tell your husband that you are a trained killer? Huh you got that man thinking he is married to a square bear boo" Ketta said as we all laughed at her she done went to Cali and started to talk like them. And that shit was so fucking funny ass fuck.

"Well honey I'm going to tell him tonight after dinner I know mom is staying with the kids so I now I will have time to really explain and break it down. I'm also going to take him to the storage I might as well get it all out because your brother doesn't have it all and is slow as hell." I said laughing and pointing at Ketta.

"Well I hope it go good for you and call me tomorrow and let me know how that goes. But don't call me tonight." Jenn said while smiling like someone just gave her a cool million.

"Okay miss thang what is going on with you?" I asked Jenn while taking a seat on the floor of my closet to take a break.

"Yeah hoe spill the fucking beans already." Ketta said adding on

"OMG! You pregnant." I yelled out getting Hella happy and shit

"Girl hell no sit your over happy ass down and wait

damn, well close yall eyes." Jenn told us while me and Ketta looked at her like she was crazy.

"For real bitch" I said

"Yes, hoe so if you wanna know close your eyes." Jenn said looking Hella serious

"Okay damn." I closed my eyes for what seemed like forever even though I think I already knew what she wanted to say but I'll go along with this lil bullshit

"Okay yall hoes can open your eyes." Jenn yelled

I opened my eyes to see the biggest fucking rock on my sis finger.

"OMG! Sis are you fucking serious right now? When? How? And where? Why am I just now knowing he asked you?" I hoped up in my sis face giving her one of the biggest hug ever.

"Well it happens the other night after I got back in town and when I tell yall this man had everything layed out to the fucking-Tee yall will be surprised just as I was I mean the dress he had waiting for me was so damn beautiful. Hell, I had to give the hotel all the damn flowers he had in my room because he had just about more than that at the house. Then get this that man had Dondria at the house singing and shit. I gave that man all of me that night. But it's been killing me to not tell yall or to wear my wing around yall. So, at dinner yall have to act like yall don't know cause he wanna tell the family all at once. I think the only person that knew was Lamar and he only knew because Ken said he felt like because he fucked up with me he needed to ask for permission from someone. And Lamar was as close as he was going to get."

"Girl I knew he was going to ask but I didn't think it would be this soon?" I said while getting up off of the floor cause my ass had started to hurt

"what you mean you knew he was going to ask?" Jenn asked looking like a lost puppy

"Well I don't know when he asked Lamar but he asked me almost two weeks ago, in the kitchen actual the same night you left his ass and we got the kids back. I told that man to get his shit together or I was going to kill his ass." I said laughing

"Well damn hoe you could have told me." Jenn said

"Girl hush your ass up at least you got a fucking ring and he did the shit the right way and for the right reason." Ketta said

"Awwwww sis we are going to find you a man I

promise." I said laughing at Ketta bitter ass

"Well yall hoes got a wedding to plan because I don't have time to deal with that shit all I wanna do is say yes and no and pick out my dress and that's it." Jenn stated looking between me and Ketta

"Well let me say this shit now yall don't need to be worried about me getting a man because I got one back in L.A and no I'm not telling yall pillow talking ass hoes shyt because I don't need Lamar nor Ken trying to kill him he is cool ass shit and that's all yall need to know." Ketta said looking serious as fuck

"It's okay sis we got you but you do have to tell us soon about this guy okay especially if you are about to be back in L.A without us or mom because you know she is not going back without the babies." I said with a serious ten in my voice so she knows I wasn't playing with her. Now

I'm not Lamar but I see what happens with that man when something happens to his family is fucked with. So, I was taking his place with this one cause when my man is not right this house is not right.

"Alright I got you sis." Ketta said

"Well let me take this ring off and let's go down to dinner yall put on your games faces." Jenn said stuffing her rock back in her bra.

I couldn't believe or be happier at this time it felt like all the drama was over. And I could finally enjoy being a new mom and wife.

Four hours later………

Dinner was finally over and the family had let expect mom she was with the kids. So, I knew it was time for me to come clean with Lamar. He was in his office so I had time to go change my clothes. I ended up putting on all white with some Vans that I had just got. I didn't need to overdo it at all since I was just going to talk to this man and take his to see all this shit I have and I'm hoping this will be okay with him.

I walked into his office to see him looking at his monitor and if I could guess what he was looking at I would say the shit from the warehouse.

"Lamar honey we need to talk can you come with me and not ask any question please." I said looking at my husband Lamar just looked up from his computer screen and shook his head at me

"Do I need my gun Anna or do you have that covered." Lamar said as he was getting up from his desk

"No Lamar but ill drive so come on." I said turning

around walking out of his office with him following me close on my fucking heels "oh yea leave your phone here you won't get service where we are going."

"Well where the fuck is you taking me and you really expect me to leave my phone here while my mom and our kids are here."

"Yes, I do because I need for you to trust me Lamar that's it so just knows that I have everything in order now can we go."

"Man, I guess." His smart ass stated as he walked out the house and got in the passages seat of my Audi truck

Once we were in the car I guess this is where all the question and I was ready for them to start coming in.

"So I know you ready to ask and I'm ready to answer and if we are going to make this work then I guess all things need to be laid out on the table." I said pulling out the driveway and heading straight to the freeway

"Well I think you know what questions I have Anna so I'm going to sit over here and smoke this blunt while you take me to wherever we going." Lamar said with his smart ass

"Okay well look some may say that I'm a trained killer but I just think if myself of a woman that knows how to defend herself at all times my father instilled certain skills in me at a very young age Lamar and I grew out that shit I didn't think a man would want a woman that could hold her on in certain situations so I let the man be the man and I stay in a woman place. But where I am taking you will shock the shit out of you."

"Anna the shit you just told me don't make no fucking since because if you were this killer then why the fuck didn't you get the fuck away from your mom then? Why the fuck did you put me through the waiting and the fucking two-million that I had to pay to get your ass back? Like explain this shit to me. and why did you decided to bring that shit out on my fucking brother Josh and his bitch?"

"Well first thing first the same way I did beat my mom ass and kill her is the same reason you let that nigga live for so fucking long. And the fact that you just called that nigga your brother is the same reason I killed his ass because I knew you couldn't and wouldn't be able to do the shit damn. And I didn't want his taking his last breath from the hands of one of your duck ass workers. And don't bring that shit my mom did to me up again. And I you want your money back I got you no worries. I didn't think you was that hurt in cash. Where you would throw that shit up in my face." I said this man got me really fucked up. I pulled off the freeway and made my way to my storage I had in the middle of nowhere.

I pulled down the dirt road and put my pin in to the gate and pulled my car in and parked.

"Anna were the fuck are we at?" Lamar asked

"Come on baby I know you are a smart man so I pretty sure you have this shit figured out already." I said as I got out the car and walked up to the wall since my shit was laid out to the max if you didn't know how to get in then you wouldn't. I place my hand on the wall where it read my hand print. While Lamar stood to the side looking on.

Once the wall slide to the side I walked in with my dear husband following behind me. As soon as I stepped in my storage all the lights came on with my walls being filled u with every type of gun you could think of. I walked of too the side room and grabbed a bag full of money. And walked back in front of Lamar and dropped it at his feet.

"There is your money back babe." I said as I walked off and sat at the table

"What the fuck!" Lamar said

"Come sit down babe let me explain this shit to you because I see you is still confused." I said crossing my legs

"Hell no! so are you some type of mob bitch or something? Like what the fuck is this shit? We are damn near out of Atlanta in some type of underground shit." Lamar said looking at the money "and where the fuck did you get all this money from"

"Well my love I have more money than I know what to do with I had this built when I was about eighteen and it wasn't hard my father had so many people around I reached out and got the shit done. And as you know the feds start looking at anyone when you have a certain amount so I started takin that shit out of my account and bringing it here you couldn't image how much money I have right now. Now I'm telling you this because I know you seen the video. And I don't want to keep this shit from you any longer." I said looking at him as he walked over to me

"How many guns do you have in here Anna? And how much money is a lot? And where do we go from here Anna? And I do apologize for bring that shit up with your mom but I see what you did on the video but I wasn't there so whatever. Will I have access to this place?"

Lamar asked

"Well first off, I have over two hundred guns in here all made for me, and I have over a hundred million in here hell daddies was giving I guess. And we go home and make love and enjoy our lives. Let's be clear about this shit Lamar this don't change anything I'm still the same woman. But now this should ease your mind to let you now that I can hold my own and that's its and all. And sure, you can have access." I said as I pressed the button under the table and seen the digital computer come alive as I set everything up and got his hand prints the same way her got mine.

"So since you have access are you cool? Are we cool now? Can we go home now?" I asked looking at him with fuck me eyes

"Yea we can go home but I'm still in shock at all this shit

but we good Ma as long as you are not out here killing people behind my back or no shit like that." Lamar said getting up and heading for the door

"Naw babe no shit like that I promise." I said as I grabbed his hand and we walked out the door with him grabbing his bag of money.

"I see you wasn't leaving that shit tho." I said laughing at his ass

"Hell, naw I'm spending this shit but look tho Ma I wanna move to L.A with mom an Ketta and just get the fuck out of Atlanta and make a new life. Like open new stores there and still have these here and still have your houses here but just start over. What do you think?"

"I love it babe when are you trying to move?"

"Hell soon, how soon can you get the house packed up?"

Lamar said as he put the money in the trunk and grabbed

the keys from me I guess he was driving

"Well hell have you found a house or something that I

should know about?" I asked looking at this man like he

was crazy

"Well no I haven't but I can get one within the next week

or so." Lamar said backing out of the gate and heading

for the freeway

"Okay let's do it" I said siting back turning up the music

and enjoying the ride. Until we get home so he can bang

my bang my back out the way I need him too matter of

fact I think I may get this party started in this damn car. I

unbuckled my pants and grabbed his hands and placed

them on my sweet spot and them him take me for a ride

on the way home.

Chapter 14 Jenn

Now that the cat is out the bag me and the girls and mama was going shopping today to look for dresses before we all move to LA. In a few weeks yall missed a lot at dinner. I'm just playing but as normal Lamar don't feel comfortable with Ketta out there alone so we all made the decision to move out to L.A. But him and Ken will still be running shit down here.

And we still have the houses out here and in LA but I have hired managers that I feel can run them and just stay in contact with us. I was ready for the move. Anna was having hell trying to pack up that damn house and find people for all them damn stores.

I can honestly say my sis has grown up since becoming a wife and mother. Now I wasn't ready for kids and Ken had me fucked up if he thought we were having kids anytime soon, maybe next year sometime. I pulled up in the parking lot where I was meeting Anna, Ketta and mom. I loved Anna dress for her wedding, so I went to the same place. I hoped out my car and headed inside.

"Hey ladies yall ready to help me find a dress?" I said to my family as I entered the store.

"Hell yeah and it took you long enough to get here, how were we here before you?" Ketta said.

"Well if you must know Ken wouldn't let me leave. That's all I am saying in the presence of my mom out of respect."

"Well thank you honey, let's get the lady so we can get this going so I can get back to them babies. I don't know what them boys is doing to my babies and I dreamed of fish last night so I don't know who or which one of yall is about to be pregnant, but beware it's one of yall." Mom said. While we were walking back I instantly looked at Anna. She was the only one getting it like that. Ken knew not to play with me.

"Well mom it's not me." I said putting my two cents in.

"Me either." Ketta said while smiling.

"Well hell it could be me. My husband doesn't understand that I don't want no more kids and we are married. So, if I am oh well." Anna said. We all stopped in our tracks and looked at her like she was crazy.

"But it's not about me and if I am or not it's about my

sister, so let's find you a dress." Anna said walking past us like she didn't just damn near admit that she might be expecting. Yall better talk to yall boy because sis is going to be pissed if she pregnant again but hey the more the better I guess.

Once we got to my room and the ladies settled in, I explained what kind of dress I was looking for before we went off to gather up a few choices. Damn near three hours later we finally picked out my dress. I chose a Swarovski Crystal wedding gown that had one of the longest trains I could think of.

Damn near the whole train was covered in crystals. I was going all out. The top was a sweetheart cut so my chest could look perfect. I had a really one of a kind dress now all we had to do was find the girls dresses that was in the color of red. Since Anna was my maid of honor her dress was different than Keta's and my mom.

By the time, we left out of the bridal store I had spent damn near twenty thousand dollars. Ken was going to be pissed once I told him later tonight. Maybe I could tell him while giving him some of this good neck action.

Well it was time to go meet my wedding planner named David Tutera, yall know him from the T.V show. I needed him on my team since the wedding was going to be in LA. I was paying for him to fly out to Atlanta so I could show him pictures of the dresses we got.

He is known to change that and he need to know that shit was paid for and it wasn't no changing so he needed to make this shit happen. Our wedding party wasn't that big but I needed a big dress just because. We all kissed my mom goodbye and the girls followed me to Chops Lobster Bar.

I wanted him to meet me there so he could get an idea of the type of food I wanted to have. I didn't want people to be Hella full were they got tired and all. I just wanted them to be ok because my wedding was going to be a party and he was going to give me just that with good music.

One hour left and everything covered with David and the girls. David went on his way and left me and the girls to talk.

"Well sis you are about to be married. You ready for this?" Anna asked.

"I don't know yall one minute I think I am and the next I'm like hell ken is a good man but is he really ready?" I said looking at Ketta.

"Why you looking at me how?" Ketta said.

"Because out of me and Anna you have known him the longest. Tell me something sis." I begged. I knew Ken, Ketta, and Lamar was Hella close because they all grew up together and they barely talked about their past, but I needed something.

"Look Jenn if you love my brother the way he is right now at this time in his life, then it doesn't matter what he used to be like and try and trust me when I say he grew up a lot and became a real man that I happen to be proud of. The people he loves, he loves and he don't want no one fucking with what is his. When Lamar use to be busy Ken use to look after me and he didn't play either. So, you have a family man on your hands and a true provider so enjoy it and don't hurt him.

For the first time, I seen a side of Ketta I was unfamiliar with and that was ok because you could tell she loved her brother and that was fine even if Ken wasn't her blood it didn't make them any closer at all.

"I got you sis you don't have anything to worry about I got him. Now onto miss maybe Prego."

"Look if I am then hell I am if I'm not then great but I can't tell my husband not to cum inside me and he want more kids so if I am then I am. I don't want to find out until we move because we all know how he can get and I got enough shit on my plate at the moment. So, can we drop it because it's not about us. Its Jenn and Ken time to enjoy so promise me yall won't say shit."

I watched as my sister gave this speech trying to get it together for herself first.

"Alright sis we got you." I looked over at Ketta as she grabbed her hand to let her know we had her back. Ketta paid the bill since Anna helped pay for the bill at the dress shop and we went our separate ways. When we got to our cars, I couldn't wait to get home to my man.

Hell I didn't want to tell them that it might be me since me and Ken been fucking like crazy. I hoped it wasn't me since I needed to go back and see my trainer Shawn when I make it back to L.A. I need to send her a message letting her know to fit me in within the next two weeks so we can get this body tight and wedding dress ready.

And I was going to be bring Anna and Ketta ass with me too when I go back hell they will thank me later.

Chapter 15 Ken

Man yall I got so much shit going on that yall don't even know how much shit I may be in. well let me catch yall up to speed so yall know that bitch that I cheated on Jenn with well she may be pregnant with my baby and I wanna kill this bitch.

But if it is my baby then I can't do that and the hoe don't want to have an abortion even tho I don't believe in them but hell my wife to be is going to kill me and her.

Hopefully I can give this hoe some money to go away

until baby is born. And then deal with it, the girls have been in L.A making the finally plans and details on our houses. We finally closed on a few properties out there me and Lamar bought three stores so we could open up our stores down there and a club as well.

The girls already have their house that Ketta and Jenn closed on a week ago, me and brody house were damn near next door now Jenn decided we need a four-bedroom with the out-door pool and shit which was cool and all because I was about to fill that bitch up with our kids.

Now the fucking over duer himself got a big ass seven bedrooms with everything they have they needed it. With how many kids this nigga was trying to have he swear Anna is pregnant.

But you haven't heard that shit from me. I was on my

way to meet up with Lamar at the shoe store to wrap up a few things there and then we needed to go pay this chick a visit.

"Hey Symore." I said as I walked into the back office and passed her deck into Lamar office.

"Hey brody what's up for the day?" I said taking a seat in front of him at his desk

"Well unlucky nigga we just have to sign all these damn papers to take Josh name off of all the properties and then sign all the papers for L.A so Symore can fax them back over today. Then we can go handle you little issue. Are the movers at your house already?" Lamar asked me.

"Yeah they got there at like seven this morning packing shit. I don't understand why we can't just buy new shyt." I said while taking a pen to sign the papers he was handing me.

"Because my nigga they clothes cost nigga the way to stay with money is to not let them spend unnecessary money now furniture they not taking that shit right. Since we are keeping the houses?" Lamar asked while handing me more papers to sign.

"She had them take a few furniture pieces that she said she couldn't live without. Man, she has a fucking list I didn't even look at that shit I just handed it over and keep it pushing. She already got me stressed over this wedding shit. Do you know how much her and Anna spent at that damn wedding shop my nigga? And that's not including the fucking wedding planner cost man." I was getting pissed all over again just thinking about that shit all over again.

"Hell I just took over and she out her spending money

like I'm a fucking bank with unlimited funds dammit."

"Man shut your cheap ass up and yea I know how much they spent I had gave Anna some money before they left to help with the cost and before you say anything fucking thing. I only did it because they don't have a father that should be paying for shit like this. So the dream wedding any woman want our women can't have that shyt so if it cost a few extra dollars so what my nigga. You know how to get it back and your stingy ass got way too much money than you know what to do with so stop being so selfish. With your future wife and my sister hell with this new dumb shit. You need to call her and give her a few extra thousands just because you know you've fucked up my nigga, Man you Hella funny Ken." Lamar said while laughing at me

I watch this nigga really laugh at my ass, and he had a

point we killed they daddy at least I could do is give her the wedding and house she wants.

"And nigga if you don't I really don't have too because her sister got money by the fucking boat loads so trust me she will get what she wants no matter what." Lamar said

"What the fuck you mean?" I asked looking confused

"Anna took me to some storage she got and have over a hundred million in there and that's not including the gun's bro she said she can kill with her bare hands bro my wife is a trained killer and I'm just now finding out." Lamar said sitting back in his chair

"Are you fucking serious right now?" I asked once again

"Nigga do it look like I'm playing so when I say they don't need us for shit and I mean that they don't need us for shit."

"Well I'll be dammed, aint that some crazy ass shit. But at least you are finding out now. But let's go and handle this business and you now we have to go get our taxes before we hop on this plane tonight."

"Yeah I know so let's go get this work done so we can head out."

Twenty min later we hopped in his car because I hated driving in this city.

"So, where too lil bro?" Lamar asked pulling out the parking lot.

"Head on over to the east side projects." I said putting my head down.

"Are you fucking serious right now you almost lost your woman and the key word is WOMAN! Over a chick that shop at Rainbow my nigga!" Lamar said with so much disappointment laced in his voice.

"Look I know okay I'm dealing with it okay. I don't need that shit from you right now let's go drop off this money so I can move on damn bro. While you over here riding for Jenn Hella hard the last time I checked nigga you were my fucking bro first." I said while sending Jenn a text message. I really felt fucked up for not letting her know what's up from the beginning.

Ken: hey baby I just wanted to let you know that I love you and I'll be there tonight. And I appreciate you taking me back. Me and Lamar is out getting everything in order I'll see you soon keep that shit wet for me.

Once I seen we was close by I called her and told her to have her ass outside in the back I didn't need no one seeing me with her ass.

"Pull in the back of these apartments right here bro and unlock the doors I'm not getting out of this car I don't want to be seen with this hoe."

"Oh, now you don't want to be seen with her or deal with her okay well look give me the money and let me show your ass how this is going to work." Lamar said as he parked the car.

Yall now this nigga has no sense what so fucking ever but at this point I don't have shyt to lose. I've tried everything and she called my bluff so hell I reached into my back pocket and gave him the money. Which was ten grands which is half of what I was giving her ungrateful ass until I find out if the baby is mine or not.

"Don't say shit to her at all bro you hear me let me do all the talking hell don't even look at the bitch." Lamar said unlocking the doors and unbuckling his seat belt.

"Alright." I said turning my phone off I didn't need to slip up and call nobody at all. As soon as I said that shit the back door to the car opened and she hopped her ragged ass in the car.

"Lil ghost what's up, bout time you got here I got shit to do." This bitch Rachel said.

"Look here hoe." Lamar said turning around in his seat with his forty-five pointed in her face.

"Don't talk to that nigga no more here is the money now this is what you are going to do first off Lil Ghost don't fucking exist to you, you never meet this nigga right here, forget his name, what he looks like, and all that shit. Second off let me see your phone unlock it too and hand that bitch over, hey brody go through it and delete everything that has to do with you pictures and texts calls and everything. Now here is half of the money I suggest you take it and do something with it here is a card when you go in labor call it and the test will be done at that time. If you fail to do so then I will have you picked up at that hospital and have you killed and trust me, you can't hide from me okay. Then I'll do the test myself and you better hope the baby belongs to my brother. If you try to contact him from this moment on I will have you snatched up and locked up until you have that baby. So think wisely okay. Now here is your phone ill have eyes on you and I know everything about you, your family and that fuck nigga you are fucking with so try me if you want to. Now do you understand?" He said while clocking the gun so she could have a better understanding.

"Yeah." I heard her say sounding like tears were running down her face.

"Okay well what are you waiting for get your dirty ass out my fucking car." Lamar said unlocking the doors again

Damn I kind of felt like a lil bitch letting this nigga handle my shit for me but he was right about so much shit I just followed his lead, I'm my brother's keeper so I knew I didn't have shyt to worry about.

"Now where is this tax shop at so we can get that over with?" Lamar said while pulling off.

"Nigga you are certified crazy I swear you are and its attached to the mall my nigga."

"Alright bet."

We rode in silence the rest of the way to the mall with us passing a blunt between the two of us and me texting Jenn here and there she was sending me Hella details about the flights and the house with Hella pictures of the house it was coming along very nice with the furniture she had there, I couldn't wait until I got there tonight damn I miss her ass.

"Alright nigga you out your feelings and thoughts and shit lets go pay for this unnecessary shyt" Mar said stepping out the car and coking the doors while he was at it.

"Alight bet I'm just ready to get out this fuck ass city I went and checked all the traps before I came to you and set all that shit up so we don't have to worry about that. I put that nigga Ernest and Tank in charge and split everything down the middle even the workers."

"See that's why I put you in charge you did good." Lamar said

"Hey brody about that I just wanna say I really appreciate you trusting me with this shit." I said as we walked into the tax shop

"Look you deserve it and there is nobody else I trust with my life more than you now get the fuck out of your feelings and let's get this shit done we only have three hours let to make it to the airport."

Fourth minutes later we were pulling back up to the store.

"Alright Mar I'll see you at your house in about thirty minutes." I said while hoping out the car to go get all my luggage from the house and headed over to his house so we could fly out together and they were picking up my car from his house too.

About an hour later I was pulling into Lamar driveway the truck was there picking up the cars and the moves were long gone, he only left one car here and that was his old Audi that was in the garage.

"You ready nigga." Lamar asked me as he walked out the house with symore behind him I guess she was our ride to the airport or something because I wasn't understanding why she wasn't here.

"Hell, yeah let's do this I need my dick wet by the morning." I said laughing

"See that's your fucking problem nigga." Lamar said hoping in the front of symore car while I put my shit in the back and hoped in the back seat "Whatever nigga I know you ready to get to your WIFE!" I said so she could hear me.

"Yea nigga I am." Lamar said

Well hell the car ride was cool we smoked out her car out

on the way there tho. Because there was no way I was

getting on that fucking plane sober.

Chapter 16 Anna

Well as yall know we are now living in freaking L.A. I must say I'm happy to get the fuck out of Atlanta. But I'm going to miss that city, but we still had so much to do until we were settled in we had two houses out here ready for kids to be moved into.

I had to go down to the state to get the rest of the paper working so that could be done. Thankful Ketta already started doing it so there isn't too much left to do. And now that Lamar is here he is handling everything for their stores. He is opening and the club I can't wait for that to be done, on top of all of that we have Jenn wedding day approaching like water on rice So I needed to get that finished.

But first thing first I had a doctor appointment today in about two hours and since I wasn't used to driving here I called a car service since Lamar wouldn't let me use uber or lyft. So, it was his way or the highway and I didn't need that nigga in my everyday business any more than he is.

I walked into Lamar office. "hey babe the car is about to pull up I'm going to stop and get Jenn and then go to all of my appointments okay the kids are with mom and the nanny upstairs I told them don't bother you and to call me if anything happens." I said all in one breath I think.

"Well damn did you breathe lol and okay just let me

know you cool and I'll see you later on babe come and give me a kiss."

I felt my phone vibrate in my purse. "look babe just a kiss the car just got here okay." I said as I walked over to my man that was sitting behind his desk with his shirt off and all his tattoos on displace that made my pussy jump just at the sight of him.

"Man, whatever come the fuck here already before I eat your pussy and really make you late." He said as I rushed my ass over to him just so I could get out the house.

I went over to my man and planted a big ass kiss on his lips so he can have something to think about later on and I made sure to suck the shit out of his tongue since he wanted to play with people.

"Damn Ma don't be kissing me like that you won't make

it out of this house and play with it if you want to."
Lamar said slapping me on my ass as I walked away.

"Is that right well then let me go before I have you eating
this full course meal over here." I said as I grabbed my
bag off of his desk and made my way to the car. And
made sure I put a lil extra dip in my walk.

Once I got in the car I gave the driver all of the address I
was going for the day and the first stop was Jenn lazy as
she could of meet me here at the house. I called Jenn and
told her to have her ass outside since we weren't that far.
Five minutes later we pulled up and she hopped her loud
ass in the car on the phone. Talking about that damn
wedding I swear this is all she talked about these last few
days and weeks.

I told the driver we could go to the next address so we
could be on our way and since my sis was on the phone

planning the wedding for the entire world not to see lol I zoned into my phone and got some shyt done.

By the time, I looked up we was pulling up into the parking lot of the doctor office. I put my phone in my purse and let the man know I'll should be done in about an hour or so. While me and Jenn got out the car.

"So sis you ready to find out if you pregnant or not?" Jenn asked me while smiling Hella hard and shit.

"Hell, yeah and I don't see what the fuck is so funny you do realize I just had a set of twins when I don't even know how that happen because I'm not a twin and neither is Lamar that I know of so it will be just my luck that I'm having twins again and if I'm pregnant and if I am Lamar will be upgrading my damn ring dammit cause I didn't sign up for this shit." I said while walking into the office and checking in while Jenn got us a few seats against the wall. My doctor in Atlanta told me to come here so I knew they had all of my files sent over already. Because I needed the best doctor in my cookie box honey.

"Well I hope you are honey I know you may not want anymore but your man wants a fucking football team and he want them close in age too." Jenn said looking up from her phone for a second

"Well damn how do you know?" I asked

"Because you man talks to my man clearly." Jenn said rolling her eyes at me

"Mrs. Williams." I heard my name called and I looked over and seen this lil cute chick with short hair and with the cutest body ever If I was into chicks she would be my type all day long lol.

"Yes, that's me." I said while me and Jenn walked up to her by the desk

"Hello my name is Deja and I'll be your nurse and I'll be taking you to your room and I will also be needed a urine sample if you don't mine. The bathroom is located down the hall on your right. Your family can wait inside the room until you get done." She said and she sounded so dam polite.

"Okay thank you here Jenn take my purse and I'll be right back." I said while walking off.

Once I made it back to the room so now at this point it was just a waiting game. Until the damn doctor found her way in here. Swear I think they make you wait in here while they talk shit about you. Yall I be tripping for no damn reason.

(KNOCK, KNOCK)

"Hello may I come in." the doctor said as she poked her head in the room like I was going to say fuck no come back later.

"Yes, you can come in." I said in the nicest voice I could mutter up.

"Well hello I'm miss brown I'll be your doctor and I received your files from your old doctor and congratulations on the twins I seen you had five months ago, by the way. So why don't you tell me what brought you in today?"

"Well it's nice to meet you and this is my sister Jenn. And thank you, well I came in today to see if I was pregnant my husband is trying to have another baby but I'm honestly not ready so I'm hoping that I'm not."

"That's a lot and nice to meet you sister and if you don't mind me asking are you using protection or birth control at this time? And what makes you think that you are pregnant? The doctor asked

"Well no because I'm married and I don't believe I should have too and I'm just checking I don't feel any different but if I'm not then I need some birth control today." I said with Hella attitude in my voice she doesn't know who the fuck I am married too. My nigga is far from a fuck nigga so his wife using anything to stop shit that happens natural won't be happening at all and that's a fight I don't want.

"Let's see if you are let me get your results from your urine test and I'll be right back." I watched her walked out the door and I was already ready to go.

"I swear if she comes back in here Jenn and tell me I am

pregnant I am going home because I don't have time for that shit.

"The hell if you are bitch we are going to go shopping fuck is you talking about and I'm going to get something to eat and I'll call up Ericka so she can have fished up everything at the house hell that's what we hired her ass for what the fuck. Talking about you going home I know you have lost your damn mind now." Jenn said smacking her gum Hella loud

(KNOCK, KNOCK)

"I'm back well I have some news for you, and yes you are pregnant so why don't you lay back and we can take a look at the baby." The doctor said I just looked at her like she had two fucking heads.

"Anna lay your ass back and lift up your shirt dammit." I

hear Jenn say as I leaned back and lifted up my pink shirt I was wearing. And let the damn doctor put that cold ass jelly on my stomach as I heard the heart beat fill the room. I couldn't even look at the screen while I had tears run down my face.

"Can you tell me if it's just one baby because my twins were a damn surprise." I asked while Jenn looked at the monitor

"Yes mama it looks like you are having another set of twins." The doctor said as I let my head fall back on the table.

"What the fuck! I yelled looking at the monitor. How! How the fuck is that possible if me or my husband is not a twin?" I asked

"We can do a test to see if you are a twin or the father is

a twin because it has to come from a parent gene." The doctor said

"Okay well doctor can you test me and print out the pictures and how long before I find out the results." I asked

"We can know in an hour so my office can give you a call when we find out, so here is your pictures and ill have everything for you up front and I'll see you in a month checkup. Congratulation again." The doctor said as she walked out the room and closed the door while I rubbed the jelly off of my stomach to get up and leave.

"Jenn don't say shit just text Erica and let's go to the fucking mall already." I made my way out to the front to get all of my paperwork and then I headed back to the car. I can't believe I'm pregnant I just got my babies back and now I have two more on the fucking way.

We just moved to freaking California! And I'm pregnant! Yall that damn husband bet not freaking touch me at all. I'm freaking four weeks pregnant which means he got me pregnant around the time we had made up. I swear I can't deal with that man right now I just wanted a pretzel and something to drink from the mall.

Once we got in the car I told the driver where to go and just looked at Jenn.

"Are you ready to be a new auntie again bitch?"

"It seems like I don't have a choice, do I? look Anna I know your husband don't want you taking birth control but that is your body and unless you wanna be having kids on the year every year then you need to put your fucking foot down after you pop out these two sis."

"I hear you but I really don't mind having babies but if

he couldn't protect me and the kids the first time then what now, I asked?"

"Then your boss the fuck up he already knows you are more than capability of holding your own so you protect your fucking kids by all means necessary." Jenn stated

"Yes, sis I hear you." I just layed my head back on the sets and closed my eyes until we got to the mall I didn't feel like having this conversation anymore.

Three hours later walking out of the mall I ended up spending so much of Lamar fucking money he ended up calling me and asking me what the fuck I was doing. I went to kid's foot locker and bought four pair of baby's shoes and put them in a gift bag two boxes were for the twins now and the other box had the baby pictures in it. I couldn't wait to get home and tell him.

But all that may be put on hold because I knew I wasn't hearing the voice that belonged to my mother. The bitch that tried to kill me and just as I thought she was walking to car not too far off. I don't she seen me because is so she wouldn't be so fucking cool.

"Jenn lets go to the fucking car now! But don't take your eyes off that bitch."

"I already know sis." Jenn said as she was speed walking to the car. Once we got close enough the driver got out of the car to help us with the bags. I just dropped everything and got in the car I didn't the bitch seeing me. this was going to be my only chance in catching her and killing her slimy ass kids or no kids.

Hell anybody that has a problem with me will be six feet under before I gave birth again. I watched her get in an all-black dodge challenger and start making her way out of the parking.

"Driver I need you to follow that car but I need you hang back so she won't see you following you can yo please do that?"

"Yes mama." The driver said pulling out about a few minutes after her car I grabbed my phone to call LAMAR!

"Hey babe what time are you coming home? Are you already in the car and on the way?" Lamar asked

"Look Lamar I don't have time for that right now I need you to listen to me I just left the mall and happen to see my mother but she didn't see me I'm turning on my location on my phone now. So, go get Ken and come meet up with me ASAP. And hurry the fuck up." I said and before he could respond to anything I had said I had hung up on him. And turned on my location see we had iPhone for this exact reason. I looked over at Jenn and she was on the phone with Ken. "sis you got your piece on you?" I asked not giving two fucks that she was in the middle of a conversation. Jenn reached in her purse and pulled out her. forty caliber pistol. I grabbed it from her and started to make sure it was cool I didn't need shit going wrong with it.

"Bitch my shit is good." Jenn said

"I know I just wanted to make sure."

I felt the car slow down as we was coming up to a few houses. I couldn't believe here this bitch is living like she didn't fuck up my life well I hope her family is ready to die. Because that was the only option for this bitch.

"Bitch if you got my piece what the fuck am I supposed

to use?" Jenn asked

Just then the driver opened up his middle console and pulled out the most beautiful forty-five barrettes I had ever seen. And trust me I have seen a lot of fucking guns as yall know.

"Here you go lil sis this is your big bro gave this to me just in case you ever needed this." The driver said

"Well I'll be dammed." I said handing Jenn back her shit.

"Lamar should be pulling up in a few minutes now." The driver said I looked behind us and seen Lamar and Ken crazy ass walking up to the car and hoping in.

"Hey babe." Lamar said giving me a kiss.

"Hey how? Never mind it really don't matter is yall ready to go in this bitch?" I asked cocking my gun.

"Hell yeah." Was all I needed to hear as I got out the car

with the crew following behind me and my husband on

the side of me......

Chapter 17 Lamar

I can't believe moved all the fucking way to L.A and I was still having to deal with the bullshit that came along with my wife and her crazy ass family.

Anna called m talking about they were following her mom from the mall. I mean damn can't we just be happy at this point in our lives. Now don't get me wrong I love killing but I just wanted a fresh start. But before I could even make it out the door this nigga Ken trigger happy ass was waiting at the front door "like you ready big bro." ken said

"Well nigga I don't have a fucking choice, let's go." I said walking out the house and hopping in the car.

I followed the GPS to Anna location her phone was giving me. And parked behind her and walked up to her car and hopped in the back seat with that nigga Ken hoping in the front passage seat.

"Hey babe." I said giving her a kiss. She was about to ask me something but ended up changing her mind instead of just asking me was I ready.

"Hell, yeah let's go I'm ready for all of this shit to be over." I said while getting out the car me and my baby was walking side by side while Ken and Jenn took the back of the house. While my bold as wife went and just knocked on the fucking front door. While covering up the damn peep hole I swear who the fuck am I really married too yall. At times this woman in front of me shock the shit out of me. I just looked at her and her eyes were black as charcoal and her soul seemed to disappear before my eyes.

"I swear we need to talk about a few things when we get home Ma." I said as she knocked on the door this time even harder.

(KNOCK, KNOCK)

"Who the fuck is at my damn door?" her mom yelled out as it sounder she was walking to the door. As soon as she opened it up which was a mistake because Anna slapped the shit out of her with the end of her gun and opened up her face between her eyes. I heard Ken and Jenn coming through the back door dragging someone with them.

"How the fuck you find me?" this bitch asked with blood dripping down her face.

"Who the fuck else is in the house?" Anna asked not fucking playing around with her nor answering her question

"Bitch go and find out oh now you hard now huh because you married to this thug ass nigga now? He made you grow a pair of balls I see." Her mom said and I swear this bitch was trying me I really didn't have to do too much of nothing seeing that my lady was in beast mode.

"Well sis you have your answer so I guess we don't need the test results after all." Jenn said throwing a bitch on the floor that looked like her mom but just a bit darker.

"Come on Ken lets go and clear upstairs." I said making sure Anna had it down here "you got this babe?"

"Yea Lamar I got it down here just go so we can get the fuck out of here aint no telling who is going to show up." Anna snapped on me yeah it was definitely something going on with my wife and I will be finding out later on tonight but for now I'll let her have this tho.

Once we cleared upstairs we ended up grabbing all that bitch money she had like four duffle bags full of hundreds which is most likely the money I paid her ass to get Anna back this bitch is dumb as hell.

"Hey babe everything is all clear up here so top that bitch off so we can go." I said while walking down the stairs and kissing Anna on the cheek as we sat the duffle bags down.

"This bitch doesn't have the guts to kill me so I guess you will have to do it good old hubby." ....

That was her mom last words because she let off a whole clip in her head alone no body shots were given at all. Then turned to her twin sister and did the same thing.

"Since yall bitch look alike yall can die the same way." Anna said while she turned to walk out the fucking house like she been doing this shit yo. Like she didn't just committee a double murder. I swear in all of my life I have never seen someone switch on and off like Anna just did.

I told the driver to take them straight home me a Ken made our way back to our car as well with the money and Ken on the phone calling the crew out this way. Now I know yall didn't think we moved out this way without a crew. Yeah, I may be out the game but I'm still the fucking boss.

Once we got to the house Ken and Jenn made the way

home and I went upstairs to find my wife sitting in the middle of out bed with tears running down her face, her gun on her lap, and Hella bags all around her and I do mean Hella bags. I dropped the bags that had the money in them and closed our bedroom door.

"Babe is you okay? I know what you just did was a lot to deal with but you know you can talk to me right." I said steeping to the bed to sit in front of her. I watch her take her gun apart and put it back together in little to no time.

"Lamar, you know I love you but there are a few things we need to talk about and I at the end of the conversation you fully understand me and where I'm coming from and who I am.

"Okay babe you are scaring me what is going on?" I said

"Well you already know I killed Josh and his bitch

Brittney without you knowing for my own reasons that I shouldn't have to explain. Now as you know my father taught me how to kill with my hands and with a gun but I would so much rather use a gun and all this you know already know. Now I don't want to kill I don't like this part of me I don't feel like is a woman place to protect. That is a job for you to do but I will stand by your side if needed don't get it twisted. Now if you don't mind can you grab that bag please."

I looked over at the kid's foot locker bag and grabbed it and handed it to her.

"Ma you just told me all of that and now you wanna show me some fucking shoes you got for the kids like what the fuck." I said while I watched her face turn all the fuck up. She pulled out four boxes and lined them up in front of me.

"Open them from left to right." Anna said I watched her move her gun I had got her and sat in on the night stand.

I opened up the first box and it was some pink and white Nike's. "okay these are nice." I said

"Keep going Lamar." I opened the second box and it was some black and white Nike's. "okay Ma theses Hella nice." I had noticed her body language change when I got to the third box.

Once I opened it I seen a baby sonogram and my eyes lit up and got Hella big I didn't even give a fuck about the shoes anymore.

"Keep going Lamar before I finish what I have to say." Anna said

I opened the last shoe box and see the same thing. I hope she wasn't telling me what I think she is telling me.

"So, if you haven't figured it out by now then let me clear it out for you I'm pregnant again with twins and we know they run on my side of the family now. But Lamar I'm your wife but this is my body and once I give birth to these two kids of ours I'm getting on birth control period until they are at least 5 no expectation I want to enjoy our life and our marriage let's start to travel now damn I don't want to always be bare foot and pregnant. You hear me Lamar?" Anna asked

"Now is it my turn to talk." I asked and when I didn't get a respond I continued

"Baby if you wanna go on birth control that's fine with me we can find one that works for your body. And thank you for having my back and standing by myside through all of this shit. And having my kids, now about all this shit that has to do with your past it is exactly that your past Ma you dent have to change for me. I married you for better or worst so I love you no matter what. But it is very fucking sexy that my wife knows how to handle herself especially with a gun. So now just know that I will be the man you need I will protect this family at all cost you don't have to worry about that. I know I let yall get touched before but that won't happen again and I can bet my life on that. So now that I have covered everything you said will it be alright if I make love to my wife now?" I asked

"No but you are more than welcome to come over here and fuck the shit out of your wife." Anna said as she pulled her top off and let her breast free I didn't even notice that she didn't have on a bra.

Like what the fuck yall my wife body was perfect even after have twins like yall don't even understand. I had her lay down while I removed her pants and thong she had on. And speeded he legs while I went down to feast on her pussy like it was always my last meal.

"Yeah Ma let me get that shit I'm not going to stop until you quirt for daddy can you do that for daddy Ma?" when I didn't get a response I stuck my tongue all the way in her and layed with her clit at the same.

"Yes, daddy I can do that for you shit just don't stop what you're doing damn daddy." Anna whispered out

The way her voice sounds when she is ready to cum the heavy breathing and all does something to me. I removed my tongue and replaced it with my fingers and did a come her motion with my fingers while I sucked the life out of her. While she squirted all in my mouth and over my face.

"Yeah Ma that's what the fuck I'm talking about!" I pulled my dick out and lifter her legs up all the way to the point they were in her face and that exactly how I wanted that ass. As I pushed my dick so far into her as far as it could go. I'm surprised I couldn't tell she was pregnant because her shyt was so fucking juicy right now.

"Yeah daddy right there don't stop please don't stop daddy this dick feel so fucking good baby OMG I'm Cumming daddy."

She knew I loved it when she begged for this dick when I felt her walls losses up on my dick I flipped that ass over on all fours with her ass totted up and I pulled my dick all the way out. Just to push all of my inches right back in to her to hear her squeal. In pleasure to see it all over my dick. I mean my dick was coated in white shit that only made me go harder.

"Throw that ass back Ma, and don't make me do all this work come on Ma let me know you want this dick Ma. Yeah just like that Ma yeah bounce that ass, yea damn Ma I'm about to nut keep doing that shit Ma." Just as I said that shit she moved her ass and put my dick in her mouth and took all of it too like a champ while she played with her pussy at the same time.

Licking off all of her juices and that shit was so fucking sexy but I could barely hold myself up due do the shit she was doing with her mouth on my dick.

"Damn Ma that's how you feeling huh I see you yeah work that shit Ma suck that shit then." I said as I felt my nut sliding down her throat once I got myself together. Before she could move I grabbed her legs and sucked on her clit as I put my thumb in her ass until I felt her legs and body shack in my hold I had on her. And I knew just

then she would be done for a few hours. I pushed the rest

of the bags that was still on the bed on the damn floor

and layed behind my wife and pulled our throw on top of

us and held her until we both feel asleep. For once I think

everything will be okay.

"I love you Anna." I said in her ear while rubbing on her

belly

"I love you too daddy." Anna said grabbing my arm to

make sure I wasn't going anywhere………

Chapter 18 Jenn

Well three weeks later......

It was finally the day of my weeding and me and the girls were staying at Anna house. Since her house was bigger and the boys was at my house. I had the works here for the day thanks to Anna ass between her and Ken I swear I didn't have to pay or shit.

But Anna went all out for me and I couldn't be more than happier than I am right now I was about to soak in the bathtub for an hour this morning. Then I had a massage after that. Then my hair stylist Jessica got started on my hair and makeup. She had nail tech here that did my nails and shit. We had a chef here that was downstairs cooking up all types of health snacks and shits but she made sure to have my favorite chocolate covered strawberries I have has so damn many of them I was hoping I could fit into my dress still. I had been working out with Shawn since I stepped back in L.A so my body as snatched in so many ways hell mine, Anna and Keta's body was on point.

"Alright everybody I need yall to UT on your dresses we have an hour to leave the house and do pictures out front before we get to the hall." Anna yelled out to nobody because it was only us here this damn girl. But we did need to get our life together mom and Ketta went to the bathroom to get into their dresses.

And yes, I'm getting married in a hall hell my husband to

be has done too much in his life to be trying to walk into a church. It was time for me to put on my dress, the girls were finally dress and we ha thirty-five minutes left to get me together and out the door.

I stepped into my dress while Anna and Ketta zipped me up on the side of my dress. Jessica added me vail to my hair I couldn't believe I was about to get married and be someone wife. Once we all got out of the house and took a few pictures we climbed into the limo that Ken got for us, and made our way to the weeding hall.

"OMG! Yall I'm about to get married today! I can't believe it! I screamed with pure joy laced in my voice.

"Yeah bitch welcome to the club your life is not just yours any longer." Anna said while drinking some cold ice water. Since she found out she was pregnant that's all she can drink I felt so bad for my sis so I decided to make her day.

"Sis you don't have to be pregnant alone so be happy that we can go through this together within the next nine months and we can have joined baby showers and shit okay." I said

"You got to be bucking kidding me!" Anna screamed damn near hoping on top of me from the other side of the freaking car.

"Yeah bitch I am now get the fuck off of me before you fuck up my dress and yours dammit."

"I can't believe you are pregnant sis when did you find out? And how far along are you? Why haven't you told Ken yet?" Anna ran off at the mouth with all the questions I wasn't ready to be asked because I didn't have any answers for her at the moment.

"Look it my weeding day an I'm not ready to talk about it the only reason I said something is because you sitting here acting like the world is coming to an end." I said giving Anna a look like she knew what I meant.

"Okay look the both of yall we are so not doing this shit today at all okay, put the babies to the side for a minute and let's go get my new sister married to one of the ugliest niggas out in L.A" Ketta said laughing breaking the ice.

"Whatever hoe and my man is far from ugly hoe." I laughed "oh excuse my langue my mom I forgot you was in the car.

"It's okay babe yall have your fun but whatever is going on between you and Anna yall need to stop that shit at the moment I wont have it in my family at all yall hear me, now let's turn up the music and get this party started since me and Ketta are the only ones that can have a drink." Mom said

"I see you mom turn all the way up then." I yelled out as the driver turned up the music so we could enjoy ourselves. Thirty minutes later we pulled up to the building with David out front waiting on us to pull up.

"Well if it isn't my bride let's get you inside to take the rest of your pictures then get you down that ailed." David said while helping us all out of the car I can't believe I'm getting married today it still hasn't hit me yet.

"Is everything okay doing his mom get her did miss Youlanda get here safe so she can marry us? I asked while walking into the L.A banquet hall.

"Yes, she has made it she is with Ken at the moment we have less than twenty minutes to get you down that ailed so let's get a move on it." David informed me as he was handing me my bouquet.

Once we were done with the pictures we were ready to go David walked me downstairs holding the end of my dress so it would get dirty. Lamar meet me at the door before it opened for me to walk In and I almost lost it and messed up my makeup.

"You didn't think I was going to let you take this walk alone now did you?" Lamar asked me

"I didn't think I would have anyone to walk me down to him and I thank you for being here for me I really do appreciate it." I said trying not to cry.

"You know I got you sis." Lamar said as he shrugged me and started to laugh

As soon as the doors open I took that long walk it seemed

like it took forever to get me down the ailed to Ken while he was standing there looking Hella good in that all white tux damn I couldn't believe this was happening.

An hour later we were walking out that hall as Mr. & MRS Kenndrick Been and I could be any happier. When we got in the car I instant tried to jump on him. I know one thing this damn baby is making me Hella Horney.

"Hey ma calm down we got all night and plus when I'm ready to tear that pussy up I'm not trying to fuck up a dress or be in a rush. So, let's just go and enjoy ourselves for the rest of the night and we will get to that later." Ken said making Hella since

"Okay babe well I do have something to tell you and I don't want you acting Hella crazy after I tell you either okay." I said sitting next to him

"Come on Ma you scaring the shit out of me just spit that shit out already." Ken said

"Well, um I'm, well you, well we are going to be parents in about eight months." I said while looking at him waiting for a response.

"Are you fucking serious! Right now, Im going to be a fucking daddy Ma! Yeah, I knew I had knocked your ass up your pussy been way too damn wet lately, yea Ma I'm Hella happy. Damn ma when is the next doctor appointment for the baby and shit?" Ken asked Hella juiced

"It will be in the next month right now but I do want to talk about the baby I just want to enjoy our reception before our lives are consumed by our child okay Ken." I said all at the same time I kind of felt bad because I wasn't nearly happy as he was.

"Okay babe we can do that lets just go and enjoy the night with our family and friends." Ken said while sounding so bombed out.

Once we made it to our reception we had a ball partying like it was no other we had our first dance to R. Kelly Forever and it was the most beautiful shit I will ever experience in my life this man is my world and I never thought I would fall in love.

We partied all night with Keke Wyatt on the mic all night we ended up walking out of there around in the wee hours of the night thank god, our room as upstairs and we didn't have to go far because I far too loaded for that. We had to get a room here because our flights didn't leave out until the next morning we were honeymooning in the Dominican Republican.

And I could wait to lay out on that beach but that would

have to wait because all I wanted to do at this point is feel my husband inside of my walls. We got to the room and I could tell ken was about to try and break my fucking back in half just by the looks he had in his eyes.

"Baby please take it easy with me." I said as ken tossed me over his shoulder while slapping me on my ass. As he opened the door and put the do not disturb sign on while he locked it behind him and tossed my ass on the bed.

"You ready to let the hotel hear my name?" Ken said trying to sound sexy I guess but that shit didn't work at all because I ended up laughing at his ass

"Boy whatever, you play too much." I said while getting off of the bed to ask him to help me take off my dress.

Inside of helping me out of my dress like I envisioned, ken ripped it slap off!

"Ken! That dress cost a grip"

"I'm bout to grip that ass."

I giggled like a school girl, marrying my best friend was a plus, but marrying my best friend who should have been a damn comedian was a blessing.

"You a mess"

"And you bout to mess up these people sheets"

Ken said while bending me over and eating my ass, he caught me off guard but my pussy was ready it stayed wet.

"You have the best groceries I ever ate"

Before I could respond ken took 3 fingers inserting them my hot vagina, my juices drip onto the floor

"Ion waste food" Ken informed as he dove head first into

my pussy eating it from the back. He slides his tongue from my opening back to the crack of my ass and that's when I let my first nut go.

Ken knew i was ready for the dick so he flipped me over, pushed my legs as far back as they would go before digging in my guts slowly. Legs shaking toes curling but tonight has been a good night, and we're just gotten started

"I love u Ken"

"Love you more Jennifer"

Ken said with so much passion i can't help but to let a tear of love fall from my eye.

After we got done making love until the damn wee hours of the morning we barely got any damn sleep before our flights I just knew I was going to sleep this whole flight.

Chapter 19 Anna

Now yall know this has went on too damn long for yall to still be in our damn business lol. But let's get to it, why don't we, well I got my sis married an off to her honeymoon. So I did my sister duties.

Now on to different things so I'm pregnant with another set of twin's me and Lamar went to my doctor appointment to talk to the doctor about birth control and since I didn't want shit changing my damn body up like all that shit do. Me and my husband decided to get my tubes tied since I was able to get them undone. And hell that wouldn't even be hundred percent.

I told Lamar that if I still happen to get knocked up after I got this shit done then her was getting fixed period no matter what. And he was going to pay the fuck up twenty grand per kid and he think I'm playing too. But he will learn let his super sperm ass put two more kids or even one yall will be pissed because I will be killing his ass.

I was standing in my closet getting dressed for the day I had a full shit load of things to do. I had to go down town L.A. to pick up all of our papers work for the new houses. And the new cases load that we will be taking on so we will have a chance to go over everything before all the kids got there. And honestly we didn't have that much time because it was so many kids depending on us, our homes could fit up to fifteen kids per house with three kids per room. And that was a lot for us but we had houses on a lot so we could build on them. Ken mom was willing to relocate to help us with them since she had a background in this field as well.

I grabbed my all white jeans with the rips in them and chains going along the front of them and paired them with my Jimmy Choo's I just had got and matched it with a black sheer blouse with the matching bra set to go with it. I topped my outfit off with my Michael Kors watch and jewelry to match. I pulled my hair into a messy bun because I didn't have the time to deal with it and these babies were making me even more tired.

And I grabbed my new MCM Bag as I rubbed some body oil on my neck and behind my ear. On my way out the door and made my way to the kids room. Lamar was already gone for the day so I didn't have to worry about getting fifty-thousands damn questions from that man today. But he made sure I had a spy with me and that shit worked my nerves.

That is one thing I did miss about Atlanta driving my damn self around because I knew the city and my cars damn I need to hurry up and learn this city cause this shit was going to stop by next week. And I miss the food that good soul food but boy oh boy what I would do for some grits and shrimp right about now.

"Hey mom how is junior and Lela today? I asked walking in the room and making my way over to pick up my babies before I leave out for a few hours.

"Well don't you look cute today! And they are good just having some tummy time I think they are moving out the way because you are pregnant these babies are teething and trying to crawl and I think lil Lamar is going to skip crawling all together and go straight to walking, because that lil boy just want to stand up and that all. Hell im surprised that he hasn't throw a damn fit by now. And have you and son came up with names yet for them babies?" Lamar mom asked. I feel weird calling her Lamar mom since that is my mom too but anywho.

"Yes we talked about that last night we are hoping its another boy and girl and if so then we decided on Korey and Ka'Maya I think that is so cute and different. What do you think? And you really think they can tell mom"

"Yes baby girl I do and I must say those names are beautiful and im so happy that my son was able to settle down and find a woman like you I can honestly say that he loves the ground you walk on and yall have been through too much bullshit so im happy that yall made it that's all now don't let us keep you from going on about your day baby and handling your business stuff, what time will you be coming back home baby?" mom asked

"You know mom ill be back sooner than you think and thank you mom that means so much to me and I love your son so much as well and im happy we were able to get back to this place as well. But can you do me a big favor when you have time can you go downstairs in the garage and get the kids big suitcases and pack them clothes and everything else they will need for a vacation. And pack your stuff also because we are going on a trip and about to have some real family time. But don't tell Lamar just yet okay I wanna surprise him. Kk I love you babies and I love you mom." I said kissing all of them on the cheeks and heading downstairs to the front to meet my driver.

After I got settled in the car I asked the driver to take me downtown. I grabbed my phone out of my purse and called up my new assistance Shell I hired her because she was about to graduate from school with her Masters Degree and she needed a paid intern and be able to get all of her hours and have a job when she was done also and that is what I was providing for her.

"Hey Shell."

"Hello mrs Williams what can I do for you today? Shell asked me all polite and shit.

"I need you to do something for me okay. I need you to drive over to my house and pack me and my husband some clothes for a trip for about two weeks all of our luggage is in the garage we both have matching so you will be able to tell what is mine and his. Oh, and of you have questions you can facetime me or call me okay and ill pay you for your extra time when I get there soon." I said all at once gasping for air

"Okay boss is there anything pacific to wear or want packed or should I just pack all the normal stuff." Shell asked me which made me giggle a little

"Yes, pack me a lot of sun dresses and sandals and few comfy clothes with matching Jordan's I need a tone of socks ummmm let me see what else and a few come fuck me outfits with matching boots and shit im pretty sure you know how to get your sexy on I see you looking hella fly when you come to work so don't act shy when you packing my shit." I said looking out the window and hearing her laugh.

"Okay I got you boss ill let you when I'm almost done and I'm leaving the houses right now as we speak." Shell informed me as I heard her hells clicking as she walked.

"Okay well ill check in with you in a few hours kk." I said as I hanged up the phone.

Well I have my work cut out for me hell trying to plan a surprise trip for my husband which I knew if he would know about it he wouldn't let us go so it had to be this way. Which is why I'm springing this on him so he wont have the chance to say no to me which he never does but still.

So, I picked my phone right back up and and got us a private jet for this trip I wanted this to be as easy as possible and I just knew if we had to go through the airport then that would have made it all hell. I sent Ketta her new man that we meet at the weeding a time and a location to meet us at. I sent Jenn a message so she could know since they were due back from they honeymoon I doubt they come tho since she was ready to get back to the business and stuff. Lamar tried calling me but I sent his ass to the voicemail. I didn't want him asking me questions so he will just have to wait.

"We will be pulling up in few seconds' mama." The driver said as the car started to slow down.

"Okay and please call me Anna or Anastasia but not Mama okay and ill give you a call on my way out so just stay close by." I informed him

"Will do Miss Anna." The driver said.

Two fucking hours later I had I had finally had all the paper work I needed to get more kids. I just needed the construction to be done once I got outside that stuffy ass building I had hella miss calls. I seen Lamar had called me a few times I decided to call him when I got in the car. Jenn Mom and Shell called me so I went in order.

"Hey Mom you called me?" I asked speaking into the phone waiting for my driver to pull up I had sent him a text letting him know that I was ready.

"Yes baby I did I was just calling to let you know that me and the kids were ready to go. I didn't want to bother you or anything like that."

"Okay Mom I'm on my way back there to change my clothes and then we can go so ill see you in a few." I said hanging up just to call Shell right back.

"Hey Shell what's going on I seen that I had a miss call from you

"Yes I just called to let you know I'm still here waiting on you to get here and that you and your husband luggages are packed and ready I also order a separate car for Ketta her spouse and your Mom and the twins so you and your husband have your own." Shell said.

"Well thank you but we could have shared a car but that is good tho and ill be there in a few I'm getting in my car right now so ill see you soon." Once I hung up the phone I called Jenn see this is one of the many reason why I couldn't wait to get on that plane tonight because I was turning this phone off as soon as we take off.

"Hey sis." Jenn said into the phone

"Hey hoe I sent you all the information you and Ken will need to meet us and when are yall leaving again?" I asked

"We are leaving tomorrow morning so we will be touching down tomorrow night Ken wants to come home and keep working but I convinced him otherwise lol" Jenn said

"I bet your nasty ass did okay well that's wonderful and remember don't tell his ass shit don't let Ken know where yall are going until after we landed so it can still be a surprise k sis."

"Yeah, yeah, yeah, I got you sis I can't wait to see you and everybody and the kids I feel like I've been gone forever, but do Lamar know Ketta boo thing is coming? And what is going on with the business?"

"Hell no he don't know and he wont know until we get to the plane and in the air since I'm blind folding his ass lol and you haven't been gone that long bitch and you haven't missed us that much you been over there sucking on hella balls and dick so shut yo ass up lol and I got all the paper work today now we are waiting on the last few things with the construction and then we will be good to go I will bring you and ketta copies with me so yall can sign off and all that good shit okay."

"Kay well I'll see you soon then sis."

"Okay sis love you." I said as I hung up the phone

By the time, I got done with all of my calls and texts and shit we were pulling up to the house. I didn't see Lamar car yet so I knew I still had time to get myself together. I hoped out the car once Vince my driver opened the door.

"Hey I have my luggage by the front door can you load it in this car before Lamar gets here since this is a surprise trip please and in the other car can you load the kids and my m stuff please I'm going to call him now so you have like 30 min." I asked Vince

"Yea Miss Anna I got you." Was his only response so I headed in the house and ran right into Shell

"Hey follow me up to my room." I said taking my steeps

two at a time

"Hey mom im back get ready to go down to the cars im calling Lamar right now." I yelled out as I entered my room with Shell on my heels

"Is everything okay Boss?" Shell asked looking confused

"Yeah I just need to get changed real quick." I said sitting my purse down on the bed

"I already laid out you an outfit in your closet I got your pick slides with some leggings and pick shirt to match since your flight is so long I wanted you to be comfy." Shell said

"Oh okay I see you well here you go." I said reaching into my purse and pulling out my wallet and paying her or the day with a lil extra on the side.

"This is way too much I can't expect this." Shell said

looking at the fifteen hundred I gave her in cash

"Look always get paid for the work you do it is three o'clock in the day you have been working since six this morning and then came and did extra work before you got off. As a woman in this business don't let no one walk over you and always set your bar high okay and know your worth and when I get back me and the ladies will have a contract for you when we get back from this trip now let me get changed and have a good weekend okay." I said to shell

"Okay and thank you and have a good trip ill see you when you get back ill be working this weekend with the construction crew and ill keep you updated via email." Shell said as she walked out of my room leaving finally

I sat on my bed and finally called Lamar back to see what he was doing

"Hey baby what are you doing?" I asked as soon as he picked up the phone

"Hey babe I've been calling you? And I just left the barbershop getting my hair cut and I was on my way home ill be there in like fifteen min. but I was thinking w could go out tonight just me and you what do you think?" Lamar asked

"Oh okay and I already made plans for us but ill tell you later but ill see you when you get home kk bye." I said hanging up I tossed my hone back in my bag and ran to the closet to get dresses in five minutes flat and ran out the room with a scarf and ear plugs in my hand.

I gave Vince my purse to put in the car and waited on Lamar to pull up. I didn't even know Ketta and her man was here I had mom and the kids in the car thank god, they were sleep cause I couldn't take it if they were up. I seen Lamar car pulling up and into the driveway so I hopped up and out of the car to meet him at his car. As he parked and turned off his big ass Hummer.

"Whats good Ma?" Lamar asked a he slipped out the car.

"Nothing much babe but I do have a surprise for you and you have to be blind folded and I need your phone also please." I said while he was looking at me like I had lost my damn mind.

"What the fuck are you talking about you are not about to bind fold me ma! Lamar said while closing his car door and looking around. He couldn't tell who was in the other car because of the tints in the windows but I need to get him in the car soon before the twins woke the fuck up. So I knew he was going to be flipping out.

"Look bae just do this for me you know I won't hurt you

at all so can you do this for me please." Lamar just look at me for a second.

"Alright Ma but look don't start with that bullshit tho." Lamar said handing me his phone.

I handed him the scarf to tie around his eyes because my short ass couldn't reach that high and then I took him by the hands and lead him to the car. I sat him in the far rear seats because I had a plan for his ass. Some would call me a freak but only with the right person I already had his blunt rolled up for him in the car and waiting.

Once we were seated in the car the driver pulled off on the way t tge plane with the second car following behind us.

"Okay babe we will be to the first place of our destination but I have a blunt for you and a lil surprise too so just sit back and go with the flow okay." I said lighting up his blunt and giving it right to him.

I reached my hands insides of his joggers he had on and pulled out his dick that looked like a hot link at this moment.

"Aye Ma what the fuck you doing?" Lamar asked

"Im doing me so just relax." I said sliding in between his legs as I wrapped my lips around his dick and played with the tip of dick where all the sensation was anyway.

"Damn ma stop playing with that shit and really get nasty with it already." I heard Lamar say as I deep throated his dick as it was growing inside my mouth as I slipped and sucked all over his dick until I felt nut slide down back of my throat.

"Damn daddy you taste so fucking good, I said as I got

up and removed my leggings I had on and slide down his dick ever so slowly as he felt all of me up.

"You thought that was your only treat for this car ride daddy?" I asked as I kissed him on his ear lobe and made my way down to his lips as I kissed him so deep as my tongue invaded his and danced around as I bounced my ass as I was on the verge of a fat ass orgasm.

"Baby I'm about to cum daddy, oh shit!" I said as I broke our kiss Lamar decided to take over as he palmed my ass and decided to beat my shit up this nigga had the driver turn up the music to drown out my fuck sounds.

"Yeah Ma take this dick!" Lamar said on the verge of nutting I could tell by the way his dick jumped inside of my pussy.

Just in enough time as we were pulling up to the air strip.

"damn daddy I don't know how I'm about to get up and move after the dicking down." I said hoping off of his dick and putting my pants back on smelling all like dick.

"Well Ma you better figure this shit out cause I'm seconds from pulling this shit off of my eyes." Lamar said while fixing his dick

"Okay babe lets get out this car and head to the finally stop." I grabbed his hand and lead him into the plane and after I seen everybody else on board already.

Chapter 20 Lamar

Anna ended up surprising me with a trip to the Bahama's with the whole fucking family. Jenn and Ken made it the next day I had to get used to Ketta new man Alex this nigga seem like he was solid but I still had my people back home working on making sure he is who he says he is. But so far so good we were finally back home and settling in to the life we have now. Anna is seven months pregnant with our second set of twins and I'm enjoying being a husband and a father. I can't believe that my life has come full circle. And me and my wife can finally enjoy our lives together.

Me and Ken is opening a new club called Twins we are about to have one of the biggest grand opening L.A. has have seen I had so many people coming out from Atlanta I mean singers rappers and the whole nine yards in the next few weeks and I could wait for that shit to open

Anna wasn't to happy about that shit she just knew I was going to go back to my old ways but hell she just had to trust me because I was more happy than I ever was so shit everything was going good now for me and mine.

I was sitting in the movie room waiting on Anna to get home so we can have movie night and shit which usually only lasted for a hour before we started fucking or she falls asleep on me. Anna insteaded on still working until it was time to deliver and she wasn't trying to hear shit I had to say period.

"Lamar babe im about to change and then ill be down okay." I heard Anna yell out.

I grabbed my phone to check all of my emails to see if I needed to approve anything. I knew I needed to send out payroll for the stores and I had a few orders going to all of the shoes stores here and in Atlanta and a few packages coming here to the house for me and Anna and the kids as well that I knew Anna was going to love.

"Hey babe what you on your phone doing." Anna said wobbling her ass over to me.

"Nothing just checking a few orders that's about it you ready to watch this movie?" I asked putting my phone down

"Yea but we have to wait for the food to get here and I

invited everyone so they should be here in a min so what movie are we watching again babe?"

"You can't remember shit babe and public enemy and why did you invite everybody we are just supposed to be spending time alone." I said pulling Anna own on my lap.

"Well damn nigga we not too happy about hanging with you either my nigga." Ken said as I turned around to see him and everybody else standing behind him looking at me with smirks on they face.

"Anna we got the food that was at the door you want me to go get plates or something and why did you order so much?" Ketta said walking and sitting the food down on the table and headed to the kitchen.

"well yeah nigga don't fault me for wanting to spend

time with my wife instead of with yall but shit yall hear

so let's start this movie." I said while Anna got up to

make her a plate of food he ass always stayed eating

something but I love her ass tho and I could be happier

right now. So my life is exactly how it was supposed to

be.

The wrap up a year later……………

Anna: I can't believe I finally had the second set of twins

so Korey and Ka'Maya was born and my house was full

and I couldn't be anymore happier. The twins have

turned one and we had the biggest party for them at our

house in the back yard we had two of the biggest cakes

that we didn't need and we got so much stuff to the point

where the kids wouldn't need shit or a while and I swear Lamar better stop ordering shit the kids had a whole room in our house full of clothes when I say this shit is crazy I mean that in every aspect .But the Sisters houses were doing amazing we were in the middle of trying to open up a few more houses the line of work that I am in I am loving it and wouldn't change shit for the world. I ended up getting some unexpected money from my father death that I didn't even realize I had coming but thanks to that no-good bastard my kids were sitting lovely thanks to him. Lamar didn't want me to take the money but I think he has figured out that I'm going to do what the fuck I please by now. But me and my click is doing good and I couldn't ask for me than that so on to the next with yall nosey ass.

Jenn: So I finally had our baby Lekenndrick junior which

I didn't have a choice in that matter but I am enjoying being a new mother and a new wife me and ken are doing great we had a lil scary time not to long ago thinking I was pregnant again so I went on birth control right away cause he had me fucked up. But I think I went overboard with all the shit I have bought lil Ken and big Ken have bought just as much as me and let's not start with Lamar and Anna crazy ass they opened up the baby an account and put half a million in that bitch I couldn't believe it when they did that shit but thy are the best god parents any parents could ask for. Married life is good and Ken hasn't left my side beside the times he has to go back to Atlanta to check on all the traps and shit but even then, I sometime go with him if I can get away from work. Speaking of which I know Anna told yall we were trying to open up more Sisters houses for more kids. We are also in the process of opening one for his mom in

Oakland that she will run for us since we are in L.A so we good over here so gone on over to Ken and see what that nigga has to say and keep his ass occupied for me for a few min or something because I can't keep his ass off of me.

Ken: look yall I'm not going to keep yall to fucking long just know that this nigga is good over here I got my lil boy here now which will was a junior no matter what. I got the traps in Atlanta bringing in more money than I can count and all the shit in L.A. the club the clothes and shoe stores I opened up with my brother but I am also opening up a chain of barbershops and a car lot I need way to clean this fucking money and I had ways to do this shit my empire will be made no matter what I have to do to get this money for my family. The lil bitch that said she was preggo by me ended up killing that baby because she knew it wasn't mine and spent that lil bread I had gave her so I didn't have to worry about her trying to expose me or anything like that. Now I know better to keep my dick in my pants or in Jenn pussy where it belongs. But I'm good over here so keep it moving your boy family is good over here.

Ketta: Little ol me is last but never least don't count me out yall just know I'm on my shit and I couldn't be any happier. I have a man that I'm so in love with his name is Alex and he treats me like the queen I am. My brother was on the fence about him at first but I think we won him over when we were on vacation. But I couldn't be happier right now at this in my life. Jenn and Anna made me a partner in the company so now I'm legit and able to say that I am the owner of something I finally bought my own house with the bonus I received when I was made partner so I am starting my own family now and enjoying life I couldn't ask to be a part of any other family.

Sneak Peek Of Check My Hustle****

By Monik & Mo Houston

Damn Bitch you need to be packing, are flight levee in a couple hours. It's money on the line. Mariah said to Ta'kia.

Ta'kia sighed heavily while going through her closet looking for the right outfits for their vacation or as Mariah would say Pay-cation.

While most people go to Hawaii for relaxing, Ta'kia and Mariah were headed out for the prostitution side. They had heard from one of their friends who is also in the game Hawaii is open for the taking.

Mariah and Ta'kia grew excited about the potential cash they would return with. So Ta'kia made sure her bag was packed and ready for when Cash and Calvon arrived to take them to San Francisco airport.

Mariah and Ta'kia had been friends since pre-k they were best friends more like sisters they did everything today. So, it was only right they get money together. Although on different teams they traveled together.

"After I graduate and get my degree I'm retiring from the game". Ta'kia said randomly while gathering the last few items she needed for the trip.

Mariah smirked and said "girl I think I'm addicted to theses free bands. I don't see me jumping out the game no time soon. I mean for what we paid are way through college, we live in the best part of Oakland / Piedmont, we riding foreign and are bank accounts lovely. Plus, we got the flyest niggas this side of the bay has to offer."

Ta'kia rolled her eyes at her best friend's outlook on things. "See Ri yeah we got theses nice homes, foreign whips, phat bank account etc. I'm just over it we went from good girls to bad bitches. We were just some squares a couple years ago, green to the game. We got involved in this shit for all the wrong reasons, to get more attention and time from Cash and Calvon and that was a joke. They were taking care of us. Only asked that we go to school, take care the house & don't be running around town thotting. I don't know about you and Cal but Cash and I relationship is damaged. Weather they say it or not they lost respect for us. You think they gone continue to wife us and we out here busting dates? Like I said weather they say it or not they lost respect for us. I can't blame them we put a price on something that was supposed to be priceless and only for them."

Mariah sat and let the knowledge her friend just kicked sink in. There was a long Silents as the girls thought about they situation. Finally, Mariah said

"Your right the other day i asked Cal to lay with me you know for some us time. He told me this ain't no boyfriend pimping and from here on out when he decided to fuck me and cuddle with me we had to use a rubber, because I'm out here fucking tricks. I was offended due to the fact I thought I was his girl and because we never used them before."

"We got to face it they lost respect for us, but like I said I will not be in the game for much longer. I been networking one of my regulars is the head of the hiring department at the law office he works at. Once I finish school he has a position for me. You got to have a plan Ri the streets don't love nobody."

Once again Mariah was speechless, although they both was about 11 months shy of graduating from UC Berkeley Mariah didn't have any real plans after. She planned to go full throttle with her hoeing. School was her backup plan in her eyes it never was a priority she simply went to please her mother and grandmother.

Chapter 21

7 years earlier

"Don't know what I'd ever do without you from the beginning to the end you've always been here right beside me so I call you my best friend" Ta'Kia ran from the bathroom after hearing her ringtone Brandy's hit single Best friend playing. She already knew it was her Best friend Mariah on the other line so she ran as quickly as she to answer before it went her to voicemail.

"Hey bitch wsp?" Ta'Kia said answering just in time.

"Damn what you over there doing sucking on some salty balls? Taking Hella long to answer and shit." Mariah said clearly annoyed that Ta'Kia didn't answer the phone quick enough for her liking.

Ta'Kia laughed and rolled her eyes at the same time and replied "girl calm your impatient as down and tell me why you called."

"Girl! Remember that nigga I told you I had been kicking it with tuff lately?" Mariah asked.

"Yea what about him?" Ta'Kia asked.

"Well he about to come pick me up to go bowling and his Patna coming too."

"Okaaaay" Ta'Kia replied already knowing where this

conversation was going.

"So I was calling to see if you wanted to come and entertain his Patna... It'll be like a double date you know"

Marian say on the other end silent with her fingers crossed hoping Ta'Kia would say yes so, she could go out with her male friend tonight. For as long as she could remember Ta'Kia was always a shy and reserved homebody. Both fresh out of high school Mariah liked to go out and have fun. Ta'Kia on the other hand was the total opposite of her bff who still stayed cooped up in the house. Growing impatient waiting on Ta'Kia to reply Mariah blurted out

"Yes? Or No? I can't keep him waiting all damn day."

"Yea I'll go" Ta'Kia replied

Shocked at what she just heard Mariah quickly said "Ok

we'll be over to pick you up in 20 minutes be ready" and hung up.

Mariah couldn't chance Ta'Kia changing her mind so she hurried and called Calvon.

"What's good?" Calvon said answering on the 3rd ring.

"Just letting you know my Best friend said yea so can bring your boy but yall got to hurry up because she be changing her mind and shit" Mariah said.

"Alright I'm with my brother right now I'm gone be pulling up to you in 10 mins." Calvon replied.

"I'll be waiting"

Click.

Just as he had said Calvon and his boy Cash pulled up to Mariah's house in 10 mins flat. He didn't even have to call or honk the horn cause Mariah was already outside on the porch.

Mariah had seen Calvon's cherry red Beamer from up the block and was ready to hop in and have him pull off. Although she was 18 and thought she was grown her over protective father would trip if he seen her get into a car with a man who wasn't blood.

Pulling up to Mariah's house Calvon rolled down the window and said "Damn babe you looking this good for me?"

Smiling Mariah replied "All the time" as she hopped in the back seat putting on her seat belt.

Calvon introduced his brother and Mariah as he pulled off "Cash, Mariah, Mariah, cash"

"Hey" - Mariah

"Wsp - Cash

"So where you say your Best friend stay?" Calvon asked Mariah.

"You know right past East Mont in them apartments next to the bank."

Alright – Calvon

Minutes later they pulled up to Mariah's Best friend Ta'Kia house. Calvon parked

"I'll be right back." Mariah hopped out the car and jogged to the door.

(Knock knock knock)

Ta'Kia hearing the door yelled "here I come" walking to the door purse in hand.

After she locked the door behind them Ta'Kia and Mariah walked to the car together. Mariah then introduced her Best friend to her male friend and his brother.

Ta'kia. Calvon and cash. Cash and Calvon my Best friend Ta'kia

Both guys turned around and said hey

Calvon pulled off and headed to a destination both unknown to the ladies.

As they rode on 580 towards Dublin Mariah and Ta'Kia both stared out the car windows listening to 106.1 kmel.

Fetty Wap's D.A.M. Song came on and Ta'Kia blurted out "this my song and started to sing."

"Your so damn fine I'm so dam glad your mines yea baby"

"Yea well you won't be hearing it today" Cash said out loud changing the station

Everybody in the car except Ta'kia started to laugh. Cash had just broken the ice being that nobody had really said a word since they'd been in the car.

So what type of stuff yall into? Cash asked.

"We don't really do much just going to school to get out the hood you know can't end up like these females out here in Oakland broke, uneducated, ran through, and hopeless."

Man that's what's up because it Aren't to many females like yall left. Calvon said.

Chapter 22

After serval double dates, and kicking it with Mariah and Ta'kia Cash and Calvon really start feeling the girls on another level. They realized the girls was more than your average hood chick they had beauty and brains.

As Cash and Calvon sat parked on thirty-eight and International smoking on cookies and listening to the latest Philty Rich album "Real Niggas Back in Style" and watching a he blades they began to chop it up.

See Calvon and Cash were knee down in the fast life from playing with sliders, pimping, and selling drugs. Since middle school they formed a brotherly bond. Both 25 and pretty successful off their street life earrings. They came from your typical single parent home and grew up enduring the struggle.

Calvon father had caught L and was serving his time in San Quentin State Prison. They hadn't seen one another since he was about nine years old. Although they kept in contact via letters and phone calls. Calvon's mother worked many jobs to provide for her children she kept their needs met not always there wants so in turn Calvon turned to the streets to pick up where his mother was lacking for him and his two younger siblings tired of seeing her bust her ass for pennies, but recently she was

diagnosed with cancer and was often too tired to work.
So automatically he took responsibility as the father
figure around the house.

Cash was the product of a pimp and hoe relationship; his
mother was his father bottom bitch back in the day. Once
Cash was born his mother left the game alone to raise
him and his other siblings his father had by a few other of
his hoes, while his father continued to travel and
continued business leveeing his mother to struggle with 3
little ones. His father sent material things or went and
paid the bills he had never actually put money in Cash's
mother hands. Which left her struggling when it came to
things they wanted to do when their dad wasn't in town.
Once Cash was old enough he took to the streets the
middle child out of him and his two sisters he made sure
his mother and sisters where ok and always kept a

thousand at least in their pocket book.

"Roll up nigga, while I go sweat that renegade over there that little red bone bitch down every night and I never seen her with no folks. You know a hoe got three choices in this here game; Choose, Lose, Or Stay Confused," Cash said while exiting his black on black Audi Q7

Calvon laughed and said "nigga you crazy, my renegade alert going off about that bitch she aint trying to elevate in this game. Do your thing, my bitches down and around twisting corners".

"Hey Handsome! Just thinking about you hoping your night is going smooth and your safe." Was the text Calvon just received from Mariah.

Almost immediately Calvon started to smile at his phone "I'm just late night trapping you know the usual if it's not too late when I'm done I'm going to pull up on you. Daddy miss you."

Mariah replied

"It's all good let me find out you really like me and daddy? Boy please, but yes pull up I'll be up studying."

"What got you over there smiling like a bitch that just robbed a trick for a Rolex?" Cash teased, they both busted out laughing.

"I aint gone lie to you brother I'm really feeling Mariah" Calvon said.

"Man that's crazy because I been meaning to holla at you about them. I'm gone make Ta'kia my bitch she solid."

"They are like a breath of fresh air. Dealing with theses

hoes all day that aint got to many ambitions in life getting frustrating sometimes. Don't get it twisted a nigga love this shit and the free bands. I love being able to sit down and have a decent conversation with somebody weather its street shit, educational or economy and bullshit Mariah can do it all. They about to start UC Berkeley that's big. That's a turn on and I want to say my bitch is educated and motivated. Considering my life that's the type of female that I would want to have my kids because if shit ever got spunky or my downfall she gone hold it down" Said Calvon.

"Brother if nobody feel you I do I'm about to go all in with it. They been rocking with us for a while now. They Hella solid to they know how we get it rather it's out a bitch ass, running in these stores or out the trap and they don't nag or bitch that's one hundred" said Cash while sparking the blunt.

There was a moment of silence while they said and reflect on all that was just said. There deep thinking was shortly interrupted by a knock on the window.

"Daddy its slow as fuck tonight aint no tricks really stopping the police got it hot from here to seventeenth. I Only made three hundred but my phone is going crazy for in-call I have a few dates set up for the next couple hours." Said Monore to Cash.

"Bitch I don't give a fuck about the police they know what's up. It's gone be police wherever you at anyways take a uber to your room you and Nana and call me when yall make it. I'll stop by to bring yall a few things from the store and yall bags." Cash instructed while rolling up his window.

"I better send my bitches an uber to it is hot as fuck out here, aint nobody trying to be bailing theses bitchs out tonight" said Calvon.

"Right I'm about to fuck around and cat off with Ta'kia after I check these traps and make sure Monore and Nana good" said Cash.

"Fo'show that's what time it is once you take me to my car I'm gone go swoop Ri and blast out the way and get a room" said Calvon.

"Cool once theses bitches let us know they made it to their rooms I guess we can swing by make show they straight , collect what they got , get them what they need for the night then I'll take you to your car" said Cash.

"Sounds good to me" said Calvon

******

Stay connected:

Facebook/ Author Monik Beene

Twitter/ AuthorMissMo

Instagram/ MissMo

If you haven't read When a thug falls for a rich girl part 1&2 please go get it and leave me your review so I can get better and give the readers what they are looking for